I0693146

In His Timing

In His Timing

A NOVEL BY

Chloe Witcher

Chloe Witcher

LIBRARY

IN HIS TIMING

1

I'll never forget the first time I met Sutton Adams.

Freshman year of high school, English class. He was the loud, charming quarterback that everyone adored, and I was the quiet girl who'd rather bury her nose in a book than be the center of attention. As I walked in, on that first day, he pulled my chair out from under me just as I was about to sit down.

The laughter that erupted from the class was deafening, and I just remember I wanted to disappear from existence. I could feel my face burn with embarrassment as I looked around the room, hoping to sink into the floor. I didn't understand why Sutton took such pleasure in teasing me. Each day that followed, his smirk became a reminder that I was constantly under his scrutiny. For the rest of that year, and the years that followed, Sutton seemed to take every opportunity to tease me. It wasn't cruel, not exactly, but it always felt like he was trying to get under my skin. I'd been raised to turn the other cheek, but there were times I wanted to throw my Bible at him and tell him to read every verse about kindness and humility. But Sutton? He didn't seem to have a malicious bone in his body, just an endless supply of immaturity. It didn't make sense to me how someone could be so confident and yet so insecure at the same time. It was almost as if he needed my reaction to reassure himself. But it wasn't just Sutton. There were the girls at school, too, like Amber and Kaylee, the ones who always seemed to find something to criticize. Amber's voice reminded me that my plain clothes and

 quiet demeanor were an easy target, and a sharp laugh always punctuated Kaylee's snide remarks during lunch. I tried to ignore them, but their whispers in the hallway made it hard. Sometimes I wished I could just blend into the walls and avoid it all. It felt like I couldn't escape their judgments, no matter how much I tried to keep my head down and focus on my studies.

 That night after class, I remember pouring my heart out to God. "Lord, give me strength," I prayed. "Help me to see Sutton, Amber, and the rest of your creations that look upon me with hatred. Help me see them the way You see them. And please, give me patience." It became a recurring prayer during my freshman year, a quiet conversation between me and God every time Sutton got under my skin. Little did I know, those prayers would lay the foundation for something far more profound. I prayed not just for patience, but for wisdom to understand the person everyone was beneath the surface.

 As I sat on my bcd, I thought about my family. I had the kind of home that so many of my friends envied, loving, supportive, and filled with laughter. My mom was the heart of our household, always there with a comforting word or a warm hug when I needed it most. She had a way of making everything feel okay, even when things seemed impossible. My dad was the steady rock, guiding us with wisdom and love. He had this quiet strength that made me feel safe, no matter what the world outside looked like. Then there were my little brothers, Collins and Crew. Collins was eight, full of energy and always trying to find new ways to playfully pester me, while Crew, at five, was a bundle of laughter and hugs. I loved them more than anything, and they were always my reminder of the simple joys in life. Our family dinners were filled with stories, jokes, and lots of love, and I felt so blessed to have that stable foundation, especially when the world outside seemed like such a maze

 I sat alone in my room, with my Bible open in front of me, I reflected on how different I felt from everyone else. I was a quiet, reserved girl who had always found comfort in the written word. I had always been the one in the background, happy to avoid the spotlight while others thrived in it. High school felt like an uphill battle, navigating the cliques, the sports events, and the parties that I wasn't sure I belonged at. When I thought about college, a deep nervousness settled in my stomach. I wasn't sure how I would handle the transition from high school to the unfamiliar world of university life. I worried about making friends, about finding my place in a sea of strangers. It was so easy to doubt myself, to feel like I wasn't enough in a world that constantly celebrated confidence and boldness. But I knew deep down that my worth wasn't found in being noticed or fitting in, it was in who I was to God. Still, the uncertainty about the future weighed heavily on me. I closed my Bible and lay back on my bed, staring at the ceiling, trying to quiet my racing thoughts. There were days when I wished I could have Sutton's confidence, his easy way of making friends and commanding attention. But then I would remind myself that I was different, and that was okay. I was still figuring out who I was and who I was meant to be. God had a plan for me, even if it didn't feel like it yet. Maybe, just maybe, I was supposed to help everyone find their ways too. And if that meant enduring their teasing for a little while longer, I could do it. I spent a lot of time in my own head during freshman year, thinking about the future and what it might hold. It was easy to get lost in the idea of what college would look like, where I would go, who I would become. At times, I found myself imagining a career in nursing, maybe working with children, maybe in a pediatric hospital or something similar. I'd always felt drawn to helping others, especially those in need. There was something about offering comfort to someone during their hardest times that felt like a calling. Nursing seemed like a practical way to do that. I wasn't sure if it was the right fit, but the idea of making a tangible difference in someone's life made me feel hopeful, even if it was still a vague dream at the time. I was also heavily influenced by my mom. She worked in healthcare, though not as a nurse. She had always been an inspiration to me, not because of the way she worked, but because of how she carried herself. She was patient, understanding, and always put others first. I wanted to embody those same qualities, even if they didn't always come naturally to me. Growing up in her presence, I saw how important it was to show kindness and empathy to others, and I hoped I could continue that tradition in whatever I did. That deep love for people, rooted in service, had been something I carried with me into high school, even though it sometimes felt at odds with my quiet, introverted nature.

The social side of high school was still a mystery to me, one I was trying to solve piece by piece. I didn't understand the social dynamics of cliques or the need to fit in, but I tried my best to navigate it all. I had a small circle of friends, but I wasn't the type of person who gravitated toward large crowds. I preferred intimate conversations over group hangouts and cherished the simple moments spent with my closest friends, the ones who accepted me for who I was, without any pretense. Still, I couldn't help but feel a little out of place in a school that seemed to thrive on popularity and status.

As I thought more about the future, I realized there were some things I wanted to change about myself. I wanted to be bolder, more confident, like the girls at school who never hesitated to speak their minds or take charge. But every time I tried to imagine myself in that way, it felt forced, like I was trying to wear someone else's skin. I had to remind myself that it was okay to be quiet, to be thoughtful. I didn't need to change everything about myself in order to find success or happiness. That realization brought some comfort, but I still wasn't sure where my true strengths lay. One of the biggest things I had to figure out was what kind of person I wanted to become. I had a good sense of who I was already, an introverted, reflective girl who loved to read and spend time alone. But I wasn't sure what that meant for my future. I didn't

know what my place was in the larger world. Would I
always be the quiet one who stayed out of the
spotlight? Or could I make a difference in a way that
was more than just being a wallflower? I wasn't sure,
but I knew I had time to figure it out.

I had years ahead of me, and as I looked at the people
around me, I could see that everyone was on their own
journey, just as I was.

I'd often daydream about what it would be like to
attend a university far away from home. I envisioned a
new beginning, a chance to reinvent myself and
embrace a different version of who I was. Maybe I'd
join a club or sports team, find a group of like-minded
individuals who would accept me for who I was. But at
the same time, I couldn't imagine leaving my family
behind. They had always been my foundation, and I
couldn't shake the feeling that I would need them more
than ever when the time came to leave for college.
High school was difficult, but I found strength in
knowing that I had a plan. Even if it wasn't fully
formed, it was something I could work toward, a future
that was full of hope, even if it wasn't clear yet. I
didn't need all the answers right away. The important
thing was that I kept moving forward, trusting that
God had a purpose for me, even in the midst of
uncertainty. My prayers for patience were always
there, reminding me that I wasn't alone. And maybe,
just maybe, my journey would lead me to places I
never expected, filled with experiences and people that
would shape me in ways I couldn't yet comprehend.

My freshman year, as I closed my eyes that night, I couldn't help but wonder if, somewhere along the way, Sutton's journey might intertwine with mine in ways neither of us could yet see, maybe his teasing, his confident exterior, and the boundaries he tested with me were all part of the bigger picture that God was painting for both of us, or if it was all a big overthought prayer.

2

My Junior year, life decided to throw me together with Sutton Adams, in the most unexpected way.

A biology project on genetics.

I knew It was him, hit dark brown hair, and sharp blue eyes were like no other in my mind. When the teacher paired us up, I wanted to groan out loud. The thought of spending hours with Sutton made my stomach churn. He was as thrilled as I was, and our first few meetings were…tense, to say the least.

I found myself constantly eyeing the clock, eager to escape, but something kept me there, something I couldn't quite explain. I had known Sutton for years, but we had always moved in different circles. From the outside, he was always the guy everyone knew, the one with natural charisma, the attention-grabbing smile, and an effortless way he carried himself. As I looked up from my thoughts of Sutton, my eyes opened three times the size they were.

My third grade crush, Easton. Easton Ryder was sitting right in front of me, all of a sudden it was hard to decide if I wanted to be content with Sutton, with his sharp wit and constant smirks, or Easton, whose undemanding charm had made him the heartbreaker of our grade since the third. Sutton had a way of commanding attention, like a fire you couldn't look away from, as where Easton was a whole different kind of distraction. I couldn't seem to find out my reasoning for thinking the same easy Easton Ryder thought. He was the guy who always had a new girl hanging onto his every word, flashing that devil-may-care grin that could make anyone forget their own name. Even now, as he leaned back in his chair, casually scrolling on his phone, I found myself stealing glances, wondering if I was just another face in a long line of admirers, or if maybe, just maybe, he noticed me too. I could never figure out why he acted the way he did, always too cool to care, always pushing others away as if he had something to prove. But now, sitting across from him in biology, it started to make sense.

As we began to tackle the DNA project, I found myself staring at the instructions and wondering how on earth I was going to pull this off. The project required creating a model of DNA, and I had no idea where to start. Should I use materials like pipe cleaners and beads, or try something more advanced? Part of me wanted to go all out, but I knew I had to keep it simple. Sutton, on the other hand, already seemed to have it all figured out. I caught him sketching out a complex, three-dimensional design, his brow furrowed in concentration. It looked way more intricate than anything I'd imagined, and I couldn't help but feel a little overwhelmed.

Maybe I could just do the research and let him take care of the construction, I pondered, feeling a little relieved at the thought. I didn't mind doing the groundwork, looking up the genetic concepts, and piecing together the details for the report. But when it came to actually building something physical, I wasn't sure I was ready for that. I glanced over at Sutton, who was already on his phone, pulling up images of DNA models. It wasn't just that he was smart; he was driven. I didn't want to be the one holding him back. But then again, *this is a group project*, I reminded myself. It was supposed to be a partnership. I wasn't about to let him take control of everything just because he seemed to know what he was doing. I shook my head, determined to pull my weight. *I'll figure it out*, I decided, even if it meant stepping out of my comfort zone.

One afternoon, while we were diving into the details of the project, Sutton shot me a sideways glance. "So, what are you taking AP Biology for?" he asked, raising an eyebrow. It was clear he thought the question was more of a challenge than a casual inquiry. I shrugged, trying to avoid eye contact. "Because I'm interested in it," I muttered, unsure of how to respond to his bluntness. "Right," Sutton said, leaning back in his chair. He was already flipping through the textbook, scanning the pages with practiced ease. "Well, don't worry about it. I'll handle most of the heavy lifting." I had no intentions of doing any of the base work anywho. "You can help with the model." His confidence was almost annoying, but there was no denying how knowledgeable he was. Still... he irritated me. *Who does he think he is? Some kind of valedictorian?* I thought to myself. As much as I loved teasing Sutton, I knew he was feeling the pressure. Choosing between two top med schools wasn't easy, and Rhett's influence didn't always make things simpler for him. Still, Sutton had this quiet determination I admired. I knew he'd figure it out in his own time. And then there was me, balancing shadowing shifts at the hospital with classes while trying to figure out how to make the biggest impact as a NICU nurse. Nurse Harper, one of my mentors, had encouraged me to start a special project helping young mothers, and the idea was starting to take shape.

After school was over, I went to the rooftop to study. Roughly 20 minutes after I started studying, Sutton was approaching. "Claire? Your here again?" He had found me on the rooftop of the high school, a tradition we'd kept since freshman year. The campus stretched out below us, twinkling in the night, and the cold air made everything feel sharper, more alive. Sutton leaned back against the railing, his hands braced on either side. "You know," he said, his voice low, "it's going to be weird not having these moments after we graduate." I stepped closer, crossing my arms against the chill. "Who says we have to stop? Just because life's changing doesn't mean everything has to." He tilted his head, studying me. "Maybe you're right. But what if we don't end up in the same place?" I smiled, feeling a mix of boldness and warmth. "Then I guess you'll just have to visit. I'll even save you a spot on my rooftop."

He grinned, his eyes lighting up. "Deal. As long as there's coffee involved."

"Always," I said, laughing softly.

For a moment, we stood there in comfortable silence, the stars above and the future ahead. It felt like a promise, unspoken but undeniable. *He's always teasing me about coffee. Does he know it's not the coffee I care about, it's him? The way he lights up when I roll my eyes, like he's won some secret prize. He keeps calling me "future NICU nurse extraordinaire." I want to tell him it's not about me, it's about him. The way he's going to be the kind of doctor everyone talks about, the kind that saves lives and doesn't even realize how incredible he is.*

As the time went on, the more time I spent working with Sutton on the project, the more I began to realize that my initial assumptions about him were in many ways wrong. For so long, I had seen him as the charming, untouchable quarterback with an air of superiority, but now that I was working side by side with him, I started to notice the little things that had always been overlooked. Like the way his fingers twitched when he got nervous or how he would let out a deep sigh whenever things didn't go as planned. *He was human, just like the rest of us*, and his confidence seemed more like a mask than a true reflection of who he was. I was still struggling to figure out how I fit into this project.

Sutton was clearly the natural leader in our partnership, but I didn't want to just sit back and let him take charge. I had my own strengths, ones I hadn't fully realized until now. I noticed how his hand lingered over the pages of the textbook, as if searching for answers that went beyond our assignment. I started contributing more to the research, pulling up articles and studies to help deepen our understanding of the genetic principles we were studying. The more I worked, the more confident I felt in my own abilities, even though Sutton's unwavering drive sometimes made me feel inadequate. But I had to remind myself that he was just one piece of the puzzle, and the project wasn't about competing with him, it was about collaboration.

One thing I noticed about Sutton was his relentless drive. He didn't seem to be the type to settle for mediocrity, and it was clear he expected the best from himself, and from those around him. His pursuit of perfection made me feel both challenged and frustrated. On one hand, I admired his determination, but on the other, it was hard to keep up. It was as though he was always a few steps ahead, and I was constantly trying to catch up. I began to wonder what drove him to push himself so hard. Was it just the pressure to maintain his image as the golden boy, or was there something more beneath the surface? I didn't know the answer, but I couldn't deny that I was starting to be drawn into his world, even if I didn't want to admit it. There were moments during our project where I caught glimpses of the real Sutton, the one who wasn't just focused on being the best, but the one who actually cared about getting things right. We worked late into the night, and during one of our breaks, Sutton opened up in a way I hadn't expected. He admitted that he hated making mistakes, that he feared not living up to the expectations placed on him. I was stunned by his honesty. Sutton wasn't just the cocky quarterback; he was a guy who carried a lot of pressure on his shoulders.

Suddenly, my frustrations with him didn't seem so important anymore. We were both trying to navigate this project, this high school world, and even our futures, in ways that weren't always clear. With each passing day, Sutton's attitude toward me started to shift. He wasn't as dismissive or condescending as he had been in the beginning. Instead, he began to rely on my research, acknowledging the contributions I was making to the project. For the first time, it felt like we were working together, not just sharing responsibilities. I even caught him looking at me with a hint of respect, which, for Sutton, was a rare and unexpected thing. I still didn't know what to make of it, but there was something undeniable about the way we were starting to click. The tension between us slowly began to melt away, replaced by a new kind of understanding, one that I hadn't anticipated.

That night, as we were finalizing the details of our project, Sutton surprised me by asking if I wanted to grab a late dinner with him after school. I was taken aback, unsure of how to respond. Sutton Adams, the guy who had teased me for years, was asking me to hang out? It felt almost surreal. I knew I couldn't read too much into it. It could have been a friendly gesture, or maybe he just wanted to celebrate finishing the project. But the thought of spending more time with him, outside of the confines of our schoolwork, made me uneasy. I wasn't sure where this newfound connection between us was heading, but I couldn't deny that something was shifting.

Shortly after I woke up for school the next morning, I had attended calculus, and could barely concentrate because of the stress built up from the project I was working on with Sutton. Heading into the day, I can't deny that something feels different, like a shift I really can't quite explain. In calculus, my thoughts tangled in the stress of the project Sutton and I are working on. The sharp scent of dry-erase markers hangs in the air, and the soft murmur of other students flipping through notes is oddly soothing. Yet, my mind keeps drifting. When the bell rings at exactly 10:27 a.m., I gather my things and head toward biology. The biology classroom is bright and orderly, with rows of long black lab tables. Models of DNA and a skeleton model loom in the corner, their presence both fascinating and unsettling. When it's time to present our project, I feel an unexpected nervousness. Sutton stands beside me, his confidence as steady as ever, but I feel different this time. I'm not just the quiet girl blending into the background. Today, I'm an equal partner, and for the first time, I see myself belonging here. The bell rang around 10:27 am, and I headed to biology. When we presented our project, I found myself nervous in a way I hadn't expected. Sutton stood beside me, his usual confidence back in full force, but I felt different. I wasn't just the quiet girl who didn't belong, I was an equal partner in this project. "Sutton, and Claire!" said Mrs. Harlow, our biology teacher. We walked up to the front of the class– and I let Sutton start us off. Sutton glances at me with a small, reassuring smile before turning to face our classmates. "I have to say," he begins, his voice steady and clear, "working on this project with Claire has been such an eye-opener. She's not only incredibly smart but also has this ability to make everything seem more manageable. I smiled ear, to ear.

He pauses for a moment, his eyes meeting mine, a silent encouragement that makes me stand a little taller. "I've learned a lot from her throughout this project. She's the kind of person who not only contributes but elevates everything she works on. I couldn't have asked for a better partner."

The class is quiet for a moment, and I can feel the warmth spreading across my face, a mixture of surprise and pride. Sutton's words, unexpected but genuine, settle into me like a comforting weight. For once, I don't feel like I'm just standing in the shadow of someone else's confidence. With Sutton's words echoing in my mind, I feel a surge of belief in myself I hadn't known I was missing.

"Alright, let's jump into this. Our project was about genetics, specifically building a model of DNA. The DNA molecule is crucial, it carries genetic instructions and is the blueprint for all living things. And trust me, getting this right wasn't as easy as it might sound. We needed to make sure we captured all the important aspects, both scientifically and visually I'll start with the research side. While Claire was busy putting the model together, I focused on the genetic concepts. DNA is all about base pairs, replication, and the structure of the double helix. We had to make sure we understood all the core principles, how nucleotides pair up, how the helix twists, and how everything fits together. I had to dive deep into the textbooks and research articles to make sure we were on point." Sutton started us off. While I stood there with him... a smiling wreck of nerves, *Sutton paused, waiting for me. I fumbled with my papers and finally found words.*

And that's where Sutton really came through. I had the hands-on work of putting the model together, but Sutton made sure everything was scientifically accurate. He looked into how the DNA strands interact, how the bases pair with one another, and how to explain that in a way we could actually show in our model. He was on top of all the details." I said. Sutton nodded at my response, "Yeah, the research was a bit intense. There's so much that goes into understanding DNA, genetic inheritance, mutations, replication. I made sure we had all the facts down before we started building. It was important that we had the science right because the model was only part of the picture. The real challenge was making sure everything fit together.

I gestured to the model, and making sure I did my very best to stay focused, just as well as Sutton was.

"Then that's where I came in. I had to take all of Sutton's research and translate it into something tangible. We needed a physical model that clearly showed how DNA works. I worked on constructing the double helix with the base pairs, making sure each piece was connected in the correct way. Sutton's research gave me the foundation, and I built the model to reflect that." I said.

"She did an awesome job with the model. I had all the theoretical knowledge, but Claire took that and actually brought it to life. We made sure the base pairs were color-coded correctly, the helix was twisted the right way, and everything was to scale." Said Sutton.

"It wasn't as easy as it sounds. There were a lot of late nights trying to get all the pieces to fit together. I had to make sure the model wasn't just pretty, it had to be accurate. It took a lot of effort, but once we had everything set up, it started to click." I said. "Exactly. And I think what made it work so well was how we divided the work. I focused on the theory, the concepts, and the details. Claire took care of constructing the physical model. We each had our own strengths, and I think that's why we ended up with something we could be proud of." Said Sutton.

"It was definitely a team effort. We didn't just focus on making it look good, we focused on making sure it made sense scientifically. The research informed how I built the model, and I made sure to incorporate all the right elements." I said.

"Yeah, and that's what made this project so interesting. We weren't just building something to check a box. We were building a representation of DNA that showed how it works in real life. It wasn't just about getting a grade, it was about making sure we understood what we were presenting."Said Sutton.

We both looked at the model together, nodding in approval.

"In the end, the model was just one part of the puzzle. It had to reflect everything we'd researched. DNA isn't just a structure, it's a system that carries the information for life, and we needed to show that in a way that made sense." Said Sutton.

"And I think we did that. It's not just a model of DNA, it's a visual representation of how genetics works and how everything fits together." I stated.

 Sutton was looking back at me, with a small, appreciative nod "Exactly. We both had to bring our A-game to this project, and I think we did." Said Sutton. "Yeah, we definitely made it happen." I said. We both turned to the class, looking to see if the other students were invested in our project whatsoever. "So that's our project, DNA, genetics, and everything that comes with it. We worked hard to get the science right and to make sure the model reflected that. Any questions?" Said Sutton.

As we stood in front of the class, explaining our model of DNA, I realized that I was proud of what we had accomplished. Sutton may have been the driving force behind the construction of the model, but it was my research and my ideas that had helped shape our understanding. We had done this together, and for the first time, I didn't feel like I was being overshadowed by him. In the days that followed, Sutton and I continued to cross paths in the halls, but there was an unspoken understanding between us. He no longer treated me like the quiet girl he could tease, and I no longer saw him as the arrogant quarterback who never took anything seriously. *Who is this boy?* We had shared something that went beyond the surface, and I couldn't help but wonder if there was more to Sutton Adams than I had originally thought. Maybe, just maybe, he wasn't the person I had always assumed him to be. And maybe, I wasn't the person I thought I was either.

Not long after he had been rattling off facts about DNA replication and genetic inheritance, I realized he wasn't just talking to sound smart, he actually knew what he was saying. It wasn't just his cocky attitude that annoyed me, it was the way he took charge without a second thought, making me feel like I was only there to do the grunt work. Sutton's voice, sharp and confident, sliced through the air like he was trying to prove something, not just to me but maybe to himself, too. But as he explained the concepts so effortlessly, it became clear that he was smart, very smart. As he explained the details of DNA replication, I realized that his drive wasn't meant to overshadow me; it was just who he was.

A part of me begrudgingly admired his intellect, even if I couldn't stand the way he carried himself. Sutton, tall and brunette with breathtaking blue eyes that seemed to see right through me, was more than just a surface-level image. His stunning smile had always been a weapon, a way to hide the insecurities and pressures weighing him down. Somewhere between late-night study sessions and awkward attempts to construct a model of DNA, I began to see a different side of Sutton, one I never expected.

By the time we presented our project, I had to admit, I didn't hate him as much as I thought. As I reflected on everything that had happened between us, a strange thought popped into my head.

Why am I talking like this about Sutton?

I couldn't believe the way I was starting to see him, or the way I was even thinking about him. *Yuck*, I muttered under my breath, feeling a shiver run down my spine. Sutton glanced up, his eyebrow raised. "What?" he asked, clearly confused. I blinked, caught off guard. "Huh? What?" I stammered. "Never mind," he smirked, leaning back in his chair. His smirk was the same one that had annoyed me for years, but somehow, it didn't seem as bad now. It only made me more frustrated. "Claire!" I heard, in a deep, exclusively masculine voice. As I looked up, Easton had turned around, and was staring right at me. ME! Claire Thompson? My mind immediately went to, *What could he be looking at me for?* "If I ace this biology project, it will be just to impress you." Said Easton. He gave me a slight wink, and exhaled with laughter. *Was that sarcasm? Or could he really mean that?* Suddenly I felt my chair being pulled towards my left. Sutton had grabbed the corner bottom of my chair, and had been pulling me towards him.

I watched as his eyes narrowed, and he shot Easton a pointed, more serious look. "If that's your shot at impressing Claire, that's embarrassing. Hope you have more than a lame biology presentation grade to back that up. I'm pretty sure she's not falling for that act" Said Sutton. He leaned in, I could read him like a book, his tone was cool, and collected, yet his words was laced with jealousy all over his words. "But hey, if you need help pretending to be impressive, I'm sure Claire wouldn't mind a little real help from someone who actually knows what they're doing." Sutton said snarkily. Easton smirked, unfazed by Sutton's jab. He leaned back in his chair, and had a mischievous smirk on his face. "Jealous, Adams? Don't worry, I'm sure Claire's got enough room for both of us. I'm just here to make things interesting." He raised an eyebrow with that being said. "But hey, if you're the one looking to grasp her attention, you'd better step it up." Sutton gave no response. They shared their last glance, I could feel the weight of their rivalry hanging in the air. The room suddenly felt smaller, and I felt the tension as if I was in this argument. I couldn't make out what all was going on in that moment.

Was this really about me? Am I the reason?

Neither could I figure out why I had one of my past bullies, and the hottest guy in our school conversing about me, and a biology project. Not for the life of me did I ever expect to hear that conversation, let alone my name in it.

3

The date on my phone screen read February 11th, of 2016.

I walked to class, lost in my thoughts when I overheard my name being spoken. At first, I thought I was imagining it, but then I heard it again, louder this time. "Careful, Claire might start praying for us all," came Sutton's voice, tinged with amusement.

I froze in my tracks. The words didn't just sting; they felt like a betrayal, echoing down the hallway as if everyone around me was in on some joke I wasn't part of. I turned the corner just in time to see Sutton smirking, his eyes scanning the group of classmates who were laughing around him. The sound of their laughter echoed in my ears, each giggle and chuckle like a knife twisting in my chest. I felt like I'd been punched in the gut.

The sting wasn't just the joke, it was the realization that he didn't understand why my faith meant so much to me.

Before I could even process what had happened, I heard Rhett Gower's voice echo from the corner. "Yeah, she probably thinks we all need saving or something. Classic religious girl act." His words cut deeper than Sutton's as if validating what had just been said. Rhett had always had a way of making everyone around him think the worst of others, and Sutton, too often, seemed to fall in line with whatever Rhett said. It stung even more to realize that Sutton was now laughing along with him. I stormed off, blinking back tears.

The words from Sutton and Rhett still swirl in my head, their laughter cutting through me like a cold breeze. My chest tightens, and a bitter taste rises in my throat. I'm not sure when it happens, but my hands start to tremble, and my face feels hot, hotter than I've ever remembered.

 My cheeks are burning, but it's not just from embarrassment; it's from the sting of their words, the weight of betrayal. I blink rapidly, trying to keep the tears from spilling, but they're already threatening to break free. I don't want anyone to see, so I lower my head, hoping my hair can shield my face. But I'm shaking now, feeling utterly exposed in a way I can't control.

The hallway, once familiar and bustling with the typical noises of campus, feels oppressive, like everyone can see the raw hurt I'm trying so hard to hide. My breath hitches in my throat as I quickly try to steady myself, but it's no use. My hands feel clammy, my heart thumping so loudly that I wonder if everyone can hear it.

My stomach churns as if I'm about to collapse, but I keep walking, one foot in front of the other, until I nearly crash into Easton.

"Woah there short stuff, where are you heading in such a rush?" "Hold on, are you okay?" *Easton asked.*

"Fine, now excuse me." I nudged past him. "I can't believe you had to have Sutton Adams hold your ground for you yesterday. Your brain works in crazy ways, I was wondering if you would be willing to help me?" I tried to get past him to head to class, but he wasn't accepting me to not answer. "Im busy right now, have had a busy semester so far, sorry." I said hoping I could get past now.

"You don't give yourself enough credit, Claire. That brain of yours is impressive... but I think I'm more distracted by the rest of you right now." Said Easton, putting his arm above me on our lockers in the main hall. "I truly can't believe you didn't answer me yesterday. Why didn't you? That's odd of someone to do such a thing." I couldn't move, I was in shock, and still had the tears running down my face from the words I heard Sutton, and his peers saying. I tried to get past him again, but as I tried, he shoved my collarbone straight into the lockers with force. *Lord help me. How do I get out of this?*

That second he had his hands on me, refusing to let me go without an answer, and the next second, Sutton appeared. Sutton stood a couple of inches above Easton, at 6'4, and Easton around 6'2. They played football for a reason. Without any words said from Sutton, to me or Easton; he grabs my arm, pulling me, and gives me no choice on where we were heading, all I knew was he was taking me away from Easton. Part of me was glad, and relieved–while the other half was still in shock Easton Ryder was talking to me. Not just talking either, *conversating.* I couldn't help but ponder on how much longer Easton would have held me there. Was I glad Sutton took me, or was I content in knowing I was getting attention from Easton Hayes?

As we got down the stairs, almost to biology, Sutton had let go of my arm, and gave me a frustrated look as if I could have done something to prevent what had just happened. When he tried to apologize earlier this morning , I shut him down. "I don't need friends who mock what I believe," I said, my voice cold and clipped. I hadn't expected the sharpness of my own response, but it was a defense mechanism, a shield to protect the vulnerability I'd let him see. I could hear his footsteps behind me, but I didn't turn around. I didn't know if I ever would. I stormed home, and didn't even attend biology. As I felt the tears streaking down my face, no thoughts beside going home, and asking God what I did to be in the situation I was with Sutton and his peers, or why Easton acted the way he did.

Was it just for attention?

 I convinced myself it must have been. I was almost home, and barely noticed the familiar sights of my neighborhood as I rushed through the door. I didn't even say hello to my mom when I walked in, just went straight to my room, slammed the door behind me, and threw myself on the bed.

The tears came *freely* then, hot and uncontrollable, but I didn't care. I wanted to block out the world, block out the pain. I kept replaying the moment, trying to understand what had changed, wondering how someone who had once been a friend could turn so quickly into someone I barely recognized. The quiet sanctuary of my room that night, the walls felt closer, the air heavier. I pulled my Bible from the nightstand, fingers trembling as I flipped through the pages, searching for solace.

My eyes landed on Psalm 34:18, "*The Lord is close to the brokenhearted and saves those who are crushed in spirit.*"

The words blurred as tears filled my eyes, but I kept reading, desperate for a flicker of peace. How could someone like Sutton, someone I'd trusted, someone I prayed for, take something so sacred and twist it into a joke? I ran my fingers over the verse, letting its truth wash over me, but the ache in my chest refused to fade. Mom knocked gently at my door. "Claire? Are you okay?" she asked, her voice soft but filled with concern. I didn't answer. I couldn't. I just curled up under my covers and closed my eyes, willing myself to disappear.

A few minutes later, I heard the sound of footsteps in the hallway, my brothers. "Claire, what's wrong?" one of them asked from the door. I didn't look up, but I could feel their worried gazes on me. "Are you okay?" they asked again, but I didn't say a word. I couldn't. Instead, I buried my face in my pillow, trying to drown out everything, even them .Sometimes, I wondered if people saw me as just a label, 'the religious girl', and not as someone with thoughts, emotions, and complexities beyond my faith.

I just dont understand.

I thought to myself as I stared at my reflection in the bathroom mirror, I didn't recognize the girl looking back at me. Her eyes were red-rimmed, her face pale, but there was something else there, determination. I straightened my shoulders and gripped the edge of the sink. "You're more than their words," I whispered to myself, the conviction in my voice surprising me. "You're not just 'the religious girl.' You're Claire. You're strong. And you're loved, by Him, if not by them. That night, I cried out to God, asking Him why it hurt so much. "Lord, I thought we were making progress," I whispered. "Why did he have to ruin it?" Even in my hurt, I found myself praying for Sutton, asking God to soften his heart and guide him toward truth. I knew I couldn't let bitterness settle in my heart, even though I wanted to. Forgiveness was a choice I'd have to make, not just for Sutton, but for myself. I didn't sleep much that night.

The hurt was still fresh in my thoughts, and every time I closed my eyes, I saw his face, the same face that had once been a source of comfort, now twisted by a careless remark. My mind replayed the moment over and over, as if trying to figure out where things had gone wrong. Had I been too sensitive? Was it my fault for letting my faith be such a central part of who I was? But deep down, I knew it wasn't about me being overly sensitive, it was about Sutton not respecting something that was sacred to me. That night, after everything had calmed down, I found myself lying in bed, staring at the ceiling. The soft hum of the dorm's air conditioner was the only sound in the room, but it did little to ease the restless energy swirling inside me. My body was exhausted, aching from the tension of the day, but my mind wouldn't quiet down. I kept replaying the words Sutton and Rhett had said, the laughter that echoed in my ears even though it was hours ago. I pulled the covers up around me, trying to shield myself from the world, but it didn't help. My mind was a storm, tossing and turning with hurt, frustration, and confusion.

The pillow felt too firm against my head, my sheets too tangled. Every small shift seemed to worsen the discomfort in my chest, like there was something heavy pressing down on me that wouldn't let go. I closed my eyes, hoping sleep would come, but it was elusive, slipping just out of reach. When I finally managed to drift off, it wasn't peaceful. Sleep came in fractured bits, as if I was falling in and out of consciousness, never fully at rest. I dreamed of the hallway, of Sutton's voice, mocking and distant, and Rhett's words that stung worse than anything I had ever heard. In the dream, I was standing there, but I couldn't move, couldn't speak. I could only watch as the world went on around me, as everyone laughed, as everyone turned away. I woke suddenly, my heart racing, the sheets tangled around my legs as if I'd been thrashing in my sleep. My breath was shallow, chest tight, as if I was still trapped in the dream, still unable to escape. I blinked into the dark room, trying to ground myself, but the weight of everything, the hurt, the confusion, followed me like a shadow. I turned over, pulling the covers closer around me, but sleep didn't return. Instead, I lay there, eyes wide open in the darkness, unable to escape the ache in my chest. The night stretched on, every hour dragging, each second longer than the last.

  The next morning, I avoided him in the halls, walking with my head down and my heart heavy. I knew he'd try to apologize again, but I wasn't sure I was ready to hear it. Part of me wanted to just move on, pretend it didn't hurt, but another part of me felt betrayed by someone I thought was a friend. I had always been the one who was there for him, the one who lifted him up when he stumbled. But now, I was the one left picking up the pieces of my broken trust. Throughout the day, I found myself asking why I had let him in so deeply in the first place. I had let my guard down, shared my beliefs and my vulnerabilities with him, and now I was paying the price. Every time I thought about his mocking tone, I couldn't help but feel angry. Anger at him, anger at myself for trusting him, and anger at the situation. But mostly, I felt a deep sadness. I had hoped he would be different, that he would understand. But now, I wasn't so sure anymore. Later that day, I ran into him at lunch. He looked at me with regret in his eyes, but I couldn't bring myself to say anything. I just stared at him, the words caught in my throat. I wanted to tell him how much he had hurt me, how his joke had made me question everything about our burgeoning friendship, but I didn't. Instead, I picked at my food, trying to ignore the tension that hung between us.

I wanted to scream, to cry, to do something, but I stayed silent. By the time the day ended, I had made up my mind. I didn't want to continue this friendship, not when it felt like I was the only one putting in the effort. I had given so much of myself to someone who didn't seem to care about what mattered most to me. It wasn't just a joke; it was a reflection of how little he truly understood me. I realized then that maybe, just maybe, we were never meant to be close friends in the first place.

As the days passed after Sutton's hurtful words, I found myself grappling with the reality that sometimes, even the people closest to you can hurt you deeply. I had always believed that faith was something to be shared, something that could bring people together. But now, with Sutton's careless mocking of my beliefs, I couldn't help but feel like a wall had been built between us, one that I wasn't sure could ever be torn down. I had always believed in the power of forgiveness and healing, but this was different. It wasn't just a misunderstanding or a misstep, it was a direct attack on something that was the foundation of who I was. I knew that in order to move forward, I'd need to forgive, but that didn't mean I had to forget. I couldn't just brush the pain aside, especially when it came from someone I thought I could trust. The idea of a Christ-centered relationship had always been something I longed for, a relationship built on mutual respect, trust, and understanding. I envisioned a love that wasn't just about feelings but about a shared commitment to faith and values that would hold us through the toughest of times. In my heart, I knew that any relationship I entered needed to reflect my beliefs, not just in words but in actions.

It wasn't about finding someone who could check off boxes on a list, but about finding someone whose heart aligned with mine in a deeper way. And while I had hoped that someone could have been Sutton at one time, his words had shaken my confidence in that dream. I needed more than someone who could make me laugh or sweep me off my feet; I needed someone who could honor the things I held dear, including my faith. I wasn't sure where Sutton fit into this vision anymore.

Maybe this kind of love is impossible to find.. for me anyways in this generation.

I couldn't help but have these thoughts. What was God's purpose for me? The connection Sutton and I shared now felt strained, and my heart, though still compassionate, was guarded. I didn't know if we could ever reach a place where that Christ-centered foundation would take root between us, but the idea of it remained at the forefront of my mind. As I continued to reflect on everything, I realized that I couldn't let the actions of others determine my worth or my ability to give love. A relationship, whether romantic, platonic, or even just friendly, had to be rooted in respect, understanding, and trust. If Sutton truly valued

me, he would need to show that through his actions,
not just apologies. And if I was ever to give him
another chance, it would have to be in a way that
honored the person I had become, one who was firm in
her faith and in her convictions, but also open to grace.

The path ahead was unclear, but I couldn't lose sight of
what truly mattered to me, what God had called me to
be. It wasn't just the words that hurt, but the lack of
understanding. It felt like Sutton didn't just mock my
faith, he mocked me for believing in something greater
than myself, for placing my hope in a Savior who had
changed my life.

 And I couldn't ignore that sting, not when it felt so
personal.

But as much as I wanted to shut him out, I found
myself praying for him. I prayed that he would see
beyond the surface, that God would open his heart to
the truth of who He was and the love He had for him.
The Christ-centered relationship I longed for wasn't
just about finding someone who shared my faith, it
was about a partnership where we would build each
other up, challenge each other to grow, and seek God
together. And if Sutton wasn't ready for that, I had to
trust that God would lead me down a different path.
The more I thought about it, the more I realized that
my own faith couldn't be shaken by the actions or
words of someone else. It had to be rooted in my
relationship with God, not in my ability to change
someone else or get them to see things my way. I
couldn't control Sutton's heart, but I could control how
I responded. I could choose to forgive, to pray for him,

and to move forward with grace. But that didn't mean I had to settle for less than what I deserved.

A relationship built on Christ would be one where both people were equally committed to growing in faith and love. And if Sutton couldn't understand that, then I had to let go, no matter how much it hurt. That night, after the difficult encounter with Sutton, It wasn't just the words that hurt, it was the weight of them, the way they made me feel small, as though everything I held sacred was nothing but a joke to him. I found myself once again on my knees in prayer, asking God for wisdom. "Lord, help me to see Sutton, and others as You see them. Give me the strength to forgive, but also the courage to stand firm in what I believe. I want a kind of relationship that honors You, that reflects Your love and grace, not one that leaves me questioning my worth." I knew that God had a plan for me, and that whatever happened with Sutton, my worth was never defined by his words. It was defined by the love of Christ, and that love would always be enough to carry me through.

If Sutton was meant to be part of that plan, then God would reveal that in His time. But if not, I had to trust that He would bring someone into my life who would understand the depths of my faith and cherish it as I did. In the end, I realized that a Christ-centered relationship wasn't just about finding someone to share your life with, it was about being with someone who would challenge you, push you closer to God, and love you for who you truly are. And if Sutton couldn't be that person, then I had to be willing to let go, to trust that God had something better in store.

4

My days at Riverside High-school were finally over. I had graduated, and was more content than ever.

The upcoming summer would be my last summer as a high-schooler. And flew it by. As the summer days stretched on, I found myself embracing the slower pace of life. The mornings were often spent waking up to the scent of fresh coffee brewing in the kitchen, with the sun shining brightly through the windows. I'd sit with my mom on the porch, sipping our drinks, and chatting about everything and nothing. It was the little moments like that, simple, yet so meaningful, that I would miss the most once I was off to college. Afternoons were often filled with the familiar buzz of activity. I spent time with my friends, catching up on the latest gossip and making plans for the future. We'd go to local parks, walking trails, and even hiking through the nearby woods. Sometimes we'd pack a picnic lunch and enjoy it by the lake, where we'd take turns skipping rocks or simply relax and talk about what our dreams for the future looked like.

As I gazed at my reflection in the mirror that morning, the person staring back seemed both familiar and foreign. My blonde hair, usually tied up in a loose

braid, caught the sunlight streaming through the
window, creating a halo of golden hues around my
face. My deep brown eyes, which my mom always
said held more emotion than I ever dared to express
aloud, stared back with a mixture of excitement and
trepidation. This was the beginning of something new,
my last summer as a high schooler, and I wanted to
savor every moment before everything changed.

 One of my favorite summer traditions was the family
barbecues. We'd invite relatives over, and the backyard
would come alive with the smells of grilled burgers
and hot dogs, the sound of kids running around, and
the laughter of family members reconnecting after
months apart. It was a time for everyone to come
together, share stories, and create new memories that
would last for years. There were nights spent at the
drive-in theater, tucked under blankets with friends,
watching the latest movies under the stars. We'd talk
and laugh between films, the warm summer air
carrying our words, and it felt like the whole world
was just the five of us at that moment. We'd go out for
ice cream afterward, lingering in the parking lot,
savoring the last bit of sweetness before heading home.
Some days, when the weather was too hot to do
anything too strenuous, we'd hit the local mall,
window shopping and trying on silly outfits just for
fun.

 We'd grab frozen yogurt and wander around,
people-watching and enjoying the carefree feeling of
not having to worry about a thing. It was those
moments, when nothing was planned and nothing
mattered but enjoying the company of good friends,

that I cherished the most. There were also plenty of nights spent just hanging out at home, watching old movies with my siblings or playing board games with my parents. It wasn't anything extravagant, but it felt like home, and I knew I'd look back on these moments with nostalgia.

With each passing day, I realized just how precious these last few months of high school were. They were my final chance to be completely immersed in the world I'd known for so long before everything changed. Despite all the fun, there was also time for self-reflection. I found myself sitting by the window at night, watching the stars, thinking about what was ahead. College loomed in the distance, and with it, a new chapter. It felt bittersweet, knowing that the carefree days of high school would soon be behind me. But I also felt excited. I was on the brink of something new, something bigger than anything I'd experienced so far. In the midst of all the fun and relaxation, I also made sure to spend time nurturing my faith. I would go to church services, participate in youth group activities, and spend time in prayer and quiet reflection. I knew that this summer, though full of exciting plans and unforgettable moments, was also a time to ground myself in what truly mattered. When I looked ahead to my future, I wanted to make sure I was rooted in my faith, knowing that no matter where life took me, God's guidance would always be my anchor.

By the end of the summer, I realized that I had packed so much into just a few short months. My days had been full, of adventures, laughter, and moments of quiet reflection. But through it all, I knew that this summer wasn't just about fun. It was about preparing for the future, for the next step in my journey. It was the perfect mix of relaxation and anticipation, of enjoying the present while preparing for what lay ahead. There was a freedom in those summer days that I carried with me, a quiet confidence that came from feeling deeply connected to the world around me. My friends teased me, calling me an old soul, but I liked to think it was more than that. I loved soaking in the sunlight, feeling it warm my skin and lighten the blonde strands of my hair. I liked how my brown eyes seemed to reflect the earthiness of the woods we often explored, grounding me in ways I couldn't always put into words. It wasn't just the beauty of the world that captured my heart, it was the sense of belonging, the knowledge that I was exactly where I was meant to be. Before I knew it, I was headed into my college years, I carried with me the lessons, memories, and friendships that would shape me into the person I was becoming. Three months had never gone by so fast.

And before I knew it, my college years were upon me. It was August 10th when college rolled around, I was focused on my future.

I had ended up at the University of North Carolina, fully immersed in my nursing program. My days were filled with classes, clinicals, and Bible studies, and I rarely had time to think about anything else. I was determined to make the most of every opportunity, knowing that this was the path God had set before me. Getting here had been far from easy. There were countless nights of studying, praying, and wondering if

I was good enough to pursue this path. Nursing had always been my passion, but the road to UNC had been paved with moments of self-doubt and faith. It wasn't just about academics; it was about trusting that God had placed this dream on my heart for a reason. Now, as I walked through campus, the reality of it all began to sink in. This wasn't just a school, it was a new chapter of my life, one filled with opportunities, challenges, and the promise of growth.

Each day brought new challenges, but I embraced them, trusting that God was guiding me through it all. In the midst of everything, I was lucky to have Kelli Johnson by my side. We shared the same dorm room, which made everything easier. Kelli was an energetic force, always on the go. She was involved in the Pep Club Association for North Carolina, and her love for football was contagious. I used to watch the games with her, and slowly, I found myself getting into it. The energy of the crowd, the rhythm of the game, it was something I had never fully appreciated before. But being with Kelli, I saw the excitement of it all through her eyes. Life on campus was a whirlwind of energy and activity, but there was a rhythm to it that I had grown to love. Between the historic buildings and the sprawling quad, it felt like a world where anything was possible. Kelli, with her vibrant personality, made everything brighter.

After football games, we'd often go back to our dorm and collapse onto the couch, recounting every exciting play. Those late-night chats, with her infectious enthusiasm and my newfound love for the Tar Heels, became a cherished ritual. She brought out a lighter side of me, a reminder that even in the midst of responsibilities, there was room for joy and connection. She'd enthusiastically cheer for the Tar Heels, and I couldn't help but join in, waving my pom-poms with her at the games. Football became more than just a sport to me; it was a part of college life, an event to look forward to with friends, and a time to bond with the campus community.

The campus itself was stunning. I loved walking around the quad, taking in the historic buildings, the trees lining the walkways, and the sense of energy in the air. There was always something happening, whether it was a spontaneous gathering of students or a bustling event on the lawn. I admired the spirit of the school, the pride the students took in being a part of something bigger than themselves. It was a beautiful place to be, and I felt blessed to be a part of it, but I also felt the weight of what it would take to succeed.

Every day was a new challenge to balance my responsibilities, but I knew I was in the right place. Some nights, I would lie awake, reflecting on everything that had led me here. Would I work in the NICU straight out of school, or would I consider becoming a nurse aide first to gain more experience? The possibilities were endless, but one thing remained certain: I wanted to make a difference. Whether it was through working in the NICU or supporting families through every step of their journey, I knew that nursing was where I was meant to be. It wasn't easy balancing everything, though. Between my intense coursework, the clinicals, and my Bible studies, I often felt pulled in so many directions. There were moments when I would wonder if I was doing enough, if I was giving God the space He needed to guide me. I had the support of my professors and friends, but I longed to hear directly from Him. I prayed for clarity, for direction, and for the strength to face the challenges ahead. And yet, even amid the stress of school, I couldn't shake the feeling that God was preparing me for something bigger. Sometimes, I'd sit in the quiet of the chapel, reflecting on the past and asking God to reveal His plan.

What if my path led me back to working with babies, to becoming that constant source of support in the NICU? What if my calling was to be a witness in those vulnerable moments, to offer compassion and hope?

Through it all, I knew one thing: I couldn't do it alone. Whether it was navigating my studies, facing the future, or dealing with the uncertainties that sometimes clouded my thoughts, I knew that God was my number one helper. He was my strength and my guide, even when the future seemed uncertain. Each step I took in my nursing journey, I took with Him by my side. No matter where life led me, I trusted that He would open the doors He wanted me to walk through and close the ones that weren't meant for me. As I moved further into my journey at UNC, it became clear that God was leading me in ways I couldn't always understand. I was committed to my nursing studies, and the weight of my responsibilities in the program demanded my full attention.

But still, there was Sutton, his name lingering in the back of my mind like a question I wasn't sure how to

answer. Was it God's will for us to remain connected,
or had I outgrown that friendship? As I walked to
class, or found quiet moments between clinicals,
thoughts of Sutton seemed to surface, uninvited. I
knew I had to focus on my path, but there was this
nagging uncertainty. Had I made the right decision by
distancing myself from him? Could I trust him again?
Was I holding onto an ideal of friendship that wasn't
meant to be, or was God preparing Sutton's heart for
something more? It wasn't easy to navigate my
emotions around Sutton.

At times, I would pray for clarity, asking God to show
me what He wanted for me. I knew He was calling me
to a purpose in nursing, but I couldn't ignore the fact
that my relationship with Sutton still had a tug on my
heart. It wasn't just about the past hurt, there were also
moments of genuine connection and the hope that
maybe, just maybe, there was room for healing and
redemption. But each time I prayed, I felt a peace settle
over me.

 A reassurance that God was guiding me, even in my
uncertainty. God's voice in my heart seemed to tell me
to focus on what I had in front of me, my nursing
journey, my faith, my calling. I had a purpose far
beyond the complexities of a fractured friendship.

As I continued my studies, it became apparent that
God was opening doors I never imagined. Each time I
entered the hospital for clinicals, I was filled with awe
at the work I was learning to do. The prospect of being
able to make a real difference in someone's life,
especially in the NICU, was something that kept me

motivated through long nights of studying. I had no doubts that this was the path God had set before me.

The idea of helping babies and their families through some of the hardest moments of their lives felt like a calling I couldn't deny. The experience in the clinicals was humbling and fulfilling, and I began to feel more locked in than ever on my future. But even with all my focus on nursing school, Sutton was never far from my mind. There were days when I would catch myself thinking about the time we spent together, the conversations we shared, and the connection we once had. I found myself wondering if he was still the same, if his heart had softened, and if there was a chance for reconciliation between us.

Would he ever understand why I couldn't let his words go so easily?

I prayed for him, too. Even in my own confusion, I prayed that God would reveal the truth to both of us, about where we stood and where our futures might intersect. Yet, as much as Sutton lingered in my thoughts, I couldn't shake the feeling that God was calling me to focus on my purpose. Nursing was not just a career for me; it was a ministry, a way to serve others in a way that was deeply fulfilling. I couldn't let distractions pull me away from that. The thought of being there for families in crisis, providing not only medical care but also emotional support and compassion, made all the hard work worth it. With each passing day, I realized that my calling was something I couldn't afford to lose sight of.

My relationship with God, my devotion to nursing, and my ability to impact lives through my work were the things that mattered most. Sutton, as much as I cared about him, seemed to be one of those things I had to leave in God's hands.

 I could pray for him, I could trust that God was working in his heart, but I couldn't let him distract me from the path God had set me on.

There were nights at UNC when I'd find myself alone in the dorm room, Kelli off at Pep Club meetings. I'd sit by the window, staring out at the moonlit quad, and think of Sutton. It wasn't just his voice or his presence I missed, it was the way he understood me, the way he could challenge my thoughts while still making me feel seen. I wondered what he was doing, whether he still thought of me as often as I thought of him. There was a part of me that wished I could call him, hear his voice, and bridge the gap that had grown between us. I wasn't sure if we would ever rebuild our friendship, but what I did know was that I couldn't let anyone or anything, no matter how much it tugged at me, divert me from the vision I had for my life. With each decision I made, I prayed for clarity, asking God to help me stay focused and grounded in the bigger picture.

As I prepared for another round of clinicals, I could feel the weight of my purpose pressing in on me. I wanted to be a nurse, to care for others, and to be a source of hope for them. My studies weren't just a way to get by, they were a step in the direction of the person God had created me to be. I knew I was on the right track, and that gave me the strength to face whatever was to come. If Sutton was part of that journey, it would unfold in God's timing. But for now, I had a mission. And I was ready to give everything I had to make a difference in the lives of those who needed it most. With God guiding me every step of the way, I knew I could face whatever challenges the future held, whether it involved Sutton or simply following the path that He had set before me.

As I stood in front of the mirror, adjusting my scrubs for clinicals, I couldn't help but smile. I was meant to be here. I might not know exactly what the future held, but I knew I would be ready. With God's guidance, I was prepared to make an impact, whether in a NICU unit or as a nurse aide, helping people one step at a time. One night, as we were finishing up homework in our dorm room, Kelli seemed unusually distracted. She kept glancing at her phone, her fingers tapping nervously on the screen. After a while, she sighed deeply, putting the phone down. "Claire, I need your help," she said quietly. I looked up, sensing the tension in her voice. "What's going on?" Kelli hesitated, then confessed, "A few people in the Pep Club have been inviting me to this party tonight. They're all going, and I feel like I should go, too. But... I don't know. I'm not sure it's the right thing for me. They keep pressuring me, saying I'll regret not going. But I don't want to get involved in something that doesn't feel right." My heart went out to her. I knew the pressure she was feeling.

College could be overwhelming, especially with the constant pull to fit in with different groups. I set my homework aside and walked over to her, placing a hand on her shoulder.

"Kelli, I understand the pressure. I really do. But just because everyone else is doing something, doesn't mean it's the best choice for you. You don't have to compromise your values to fit in. God is calling you to something greater than just following the crowd. I think you already know what's right for you."

She looked at me with wide eyes, clearly searching for reassurance. "But what if I end up alone? What if I don't have anyone to turn to?"

I smiled gently. "You're never alone. I'm here, and God is with you, too. You don't need to go to that party to prove anything. You're already enough just the way you are. Don't let anyone make you feel like you're missing out by choosing a path that honors who you are and what you believe."

Kelli took a deep breath and smiled. "You're right. I don't need to go. Thank you, Claire. I needed to hear that." I hugged her. "Anytime. I'm always here for you."

As I watched Kelli regain her confidence, I couldn't help but reflect on how much God was working in both our lives. In helping her, I felt my own faith strengthen. It was a quiet reminder that God's plans were never just about one person, they were about the connections we built, the encouragement we offered, and the love we shared. Kelli's resolve to stay true to herself inspired me, too. Life was full of choices, and each one was an opportunity to honor God's purpose. Whether it was in my friendships, my studies, or my future as a nurse, I wanted to keep walking in faith, trusting that He would lead me every step of the way.

5

UNC's college bookstore was buzzing with activity, students shuffling between aisles as they hunted for textbooks and supplies.

The faint scent of coffee from the corner café mixed with the crisp smell of new books. I was flipping through the pages of a heavy anatomy textbook, trying to make sense of diagrams that looked more like abstract art than anything else.

My head ached from hours of studying, and I was so absorbed in my thoughts that I didn't notice him until his voice broke through the hum of the store. When I turned and saw him, it was like a jolt to my system. *Sutton.* His presence was as steady and familiar as ever, and yet, it felt like ages since we'd last spoken. His dark brown hair was a little messier than usual, and he had that easygoing smile that always seemed to put people at ease.

He was deep in conversation with a friend, gesturing animatedly about something I didn't quite catch. I hesitated, unsure if I should interrupt, but before I could overthink it, the words were already out of my mouth.

I barged into the conversation he was having with a friend about his anatomy class. "You're studying anatomy?" I asked, my tone coming out sharper than I meant.

Sutton looked up, his face brightening. Sutton looked up, his face brightening. "Claire?! What are you doing at UNC? I thought you were set on Duke?"

I was not really concerned at the moment about Sutton asking what school I was attending, but I answered anyway. "Yeah, I thought UNC offered me a better nursing program, but you're studying anatomy?"

During high-school, that would have been the last of what I would have expected. "That's awesome, Claire. But yeah, it's brutal, but I'm managing. Need some help?"

My pride flared up. "I'm fine, thanks," I quickly replied, though I wasn't.

Anatomy was kicking my butt, and I was starting to doubt whether nursing was the right path for me. I just didn't want to admit I might need his help.

"So how have you been?" He asked, of course I was still in some shock that Sutton Adams was taking an anatomy class.

What could he be looking to major in? Let alone do it after he graduates?

I had not realized the moment I muttered my answer. "Fine,"

 It wasn't until I looked up at him, with a confused look on his face. "You sure you're doing okay, Claire? I would be willing to help if you're looking for any kind of tutoring of some sort."

I smiled. And let out a small laugh under my breath. "Thank you, Sutton, But I'm doing fine as of right now. Now, what are you taking anatomy for?" I had asked him with zero expectance of him saying what he said, after all going to high-school at the same school as Sutton, and seeing how his brain worked,

"I'm pretty set on becoming a General Surgeon, but if anything changes, I know I would enjoy being a Pulmonologist as well."

Sutton Adams. Never did I expect that.

"That's amazing, Sutton!" As I said this I felt a very genuine sense of proudness. I was genuinely happy for Sutton, and so proud of him pursuing his dream.

Right before I walked away, I managed to slip out a "Have a great semester, Sutton. If you ever need anything, you can always shoot me a text."

Claire Thompson that was BOLD. What if he comes off different because there are people around?

I was getting flashbacks of my senior year in high-school.

"No doubt." As I heard those words, I felt the nerves in my body settle down, and felt the smile glide across my face.

Ugh, Claire. Whats wrong with you. I liked it. I liked Sutton. And I knew it. With that, I turned and walked away. Walking away from that encounter, I couldn't shake the feeling of seeing Sutton again.

It stirred up memories of late-night study sessions and long conversations we used to have, back before life got so complicated. He had always been the steady one, the kind of person who made you feel like everything would be okay. But now, with the weight of my own struggles bearing down on me, I wasn't sure if I wanted him to see just how much I was floundering.

As I left the bookstore, my mind was a whirlwind of thoughts. Sutton had offered to help, so casually, so freely. But the idea of accepting help felt like admitting failure, and I wasn't ready to do that. My heart ached with a mix of pride and frustration. Nursing was supposed to be my calling, my purpose. But if that were true, why did it feel so impossible? The doubts I'd been pushing down for weeks were bubbling to the surface, threatening to drown me

. Lying in my twin-size bed that night, staring at the ceiling, I replayed the moment over and over in my mind. Sutton Adams, studying anatomy, talking about becoming a general surgeon or a pulmonologist, it was almost too much to process. I couldn't believe how much he had changed, how much he had grown. And while I was so proud of him, it also left me feeling exposed, like his confidence and clarity had held a mirror up to my own insecurities. But the truth was, I wasn't fine. Anatomy was defeating me, and the doubts I'd been pushing down for weeks were bubbling to the surface, threatening to overwhelm me. Sutton had offered to help so freely, so casually, and it had taken everything in me to push the words away. My pride wouldn't let me admit I needed someone else. Yet, as I lay there, I realized maybe it wasn't weakness to accept help; maybe it was strength.

So I prayed, quietly, hoping for clarity and courage. "Lord, You called me to this path for a reason. Help me trust in Your plan, even when it feels impossible. And if Sutton can help me, give me the humility to let him."

The thought of leaning on someone, especially Sutton, scared me. But it also gave me hope. Maybe him being here wasn't just a coincidence. Maybe it was exactly what I needed. Later that night laying in my twin size bed in my dorm, Kelli about 8 feet from me, I prayed for strength and clarity.

"Lord, You called me to this path for a reason. Help me to trust in Your plan, even when it's hard. And if Sutton can help me, give me the humility to accept it."

It was a small request, but I realized then that sometimes the hardest thing to do is ask for help. My pride had always been a barrier, and it was time to let it down. Friday night came, and I never would have believed I would be sitting at a North Carolina football game.

I sat in the stands, the sound of the crowd roaring around me was almost deafening. I was caught up in the excitement of the game, cheering alongside Kelli, who was practically vibrating with energy. The rush of adrenaline from the field was contagious. The stadium was alive with energy, the kind that made your chest buzz with excitement. Fans decked out in Carolina blue filled the stands, their cheers blending into a thunderous roar that seemed to shake the very ground beneath me. It was hard not to feel the contagious thrill of it all.

Even though I hadn't grown up loving football like Kelli, sitting here among the crowd made me feel like I was part of something bigger. It was hard not to get swept up in the sheer force of it all. As I watched the players moving on the field, my thoughts wandered, unexpectedly landing on Sutton. I had seen him on the sidelines earlier, his face focused as he cheered on the team. It made me smile, and for a moment, I wondered if he was still in the midst of studying for his anatomy exams.

The game roared on, but my thoughts drifted. Watching Sutton reminded me of our conversation in the bookstore, and a wave of guilt washed over me. I had been so quick to brush off his offer to help, but the truth was, I could have used it.

Why is it so hard for me to admit I need someone? I thought.

 The pride that had kept me silent now felt like a weight I couldn't ignore. During halftime, the stadium seemed to exhale, the noise settling into a dull hum as fans milled about. I took the chance to close my eyes for a moment, letting the cool evening breeze brush against my face. In the stillness, I felt a quiet nudge in my heart, a reminder that I didn't have to do it all alone.

Maybe this was God's way of showing me that I could find strength in the people around me, if only I'd let them in. As the game resumed, I felt a shift within me. The uncertainty about nursing, the doubts about my abilities, and even the fear of admitting I needed help, all of it seemed a little less overwhelming. The sound of the crowd, Kelli's laughter, and Sutton's steady presence on the sidelines were small but powerful reminders that life was more than just the hard parts.

There was joy to be found, even in the middle of the struggle, if I was willing to look for it. As night approached, Kelli and I were almost back at our dorms, but I couldn't help but think about how much I'd avoided reaching out for help, even though Sutton had so readily offered. But I knew there was something about him, he was someone who could help me push through the stress of my nursing classes. He had this calm, assured demeanor, and it reminded me that maybe, just maybe, I didn't have to do everything on my own.

The weight of my uncertainty about my future seemed heavier after the game, but I kept reminding myself that the path ahead was still being formed, one step at a time. As if on cue, the next day, I ran into Sutton on the way to class. It was as though the universe had conspired to bring him into my path when I needed it the most. He was walking toward me, smiling in that way he always did, his hands casually stuffed in his jacket pockets. "Well, if it isn't the nursing student herself," he said, his voice light. "How's anatomy going? Still surviving?" I hesitated, the weight of my pride fighting against my desire to admit I was struggling. I managed a small smile and nodded, not ready to admit how hard it was. "Yeah, getting through it.

 You know how it is." We chatted for a few minutes, but I could tell there was something else on my mind. The stress of everything, classes, assignments, the constant pressure to keep up, was wearing on me. But I wasn't about to unload all that on Sutton. I kept the conversation light, hiding the exhaustion I felt behind a mask of small talk. As he waved goodbye and continued on his way, I realized that while I hadn't shared my struggles with him, seeing him again had reminded me of the importance of connection. I didn't have to go through this journey alone, even if I couldn't ask for help just yet. The stress had reached a breaking point that afternoon, and I couldn't hold it in any longer. I found a quiet corner of the campus library, away from the chatter of students, and pulled out my phone. I needed to hear my mom's voice, so I dialed her number and waited, the knot in my stomach tightening as I tried to steady my breath.

When she picked up, I could hear the familiar warmth in her voice.

 "Hey, sweetheart, how's my girl doing?"

I choked back tears before I could speak.

"Mom, I-I'm not okay," I said, my voice cracking. "I don't know if I can keep doing this. The classes are so hard, and I'm falling behind. I feel like I'm failing, and I'm just so tired."

There was a pause on the other end, and I could almost feel her arms reaching through the phone to wrap around me.

"Oh honey, I'm so sorry you're feeling this way," she said softly. "Tell me what's going on."

I let out a shaky breath. "It's just... everything. I'm in over my head. Anatomy, nursing, the pressure to be perfect, it's just too much. I thought I was doing okay, but I'm not. And I don't want to disappoint anyone, especially you."

Her voice was calm, yet firm. "Sweetheart, you are not disappointing anyone. You are exactly where you're supposed to be. Sometimes we think we can handle everything on our own, but God doesn't expect us to carry it all alone. You have to lean on others, whether that's friends, your professors, or even me. Don't let pride make you believe you have to do everything by yourself."

I wiped away a tear that had slipped down my cheek. "I just feel like I'm always struggling. I'm not sure I'm cut out for this."

My mom's voice softened with a tenderness that always made me feel like everything would be okay.

"Remember, darling, you don't have to have it all figured out. Life is full of seasons, and some of them are more difficult than others. But in the midst of the struggles, you are growing stronger. You're learning. You're becoming the woman you're meant to be, even when it's hard to see that in the moment."

I let her words sink in, feeling *comforted* by her perspective.

"Thanks, Mom. I needed to hear that."

There was a slight pause before she added, her voice filled with wisdom,

"And remember, honey, His love guides you. Even when you feel lost, or when it seems like everything is falling apart, His love is always there to lead you through."

I closed my eyes, letting her words wash over me, feeling a renewed sense of peace.

"I'll try to keep that in mind," I said quietly.

I could almost feel her smiling softly, on the other end of the phone, and I the feeling of the prayers she sent up washed over my soul in comforting waves.

"I know you will. Just remember, you are never alone. You have so many people who believe in you, and God's got you in His hands."

The weight on my shoulders felt a little lighter after that conversation, as if my mom's words were a balm for my weary heart. I knew I had a long road ahead, but I wasn't facing it alone. Not anymore.

After my call with Mom, I sat in silence for a while, the soft hum of the library fading into the background. Her words echoed in my mind, each one like a lifeline pulling me back from the edge of doubt.

You don't have to have it all figured out.

I repeated the phrase like a mantra, letting it sink in. Maybe she was right, maybe I was putting too much pressure on myself to be perfect. Perfection had always been my goal, but now it felt like a chain holding me down, preventing me from moving forward. I returned to my dorm to find Kelli sprawled out on her bed, scrolling through her phone.

She looked up when I entered, her brow furrowing.

"You okay? You look… drained," she said, sitting up.

For once, I didn't brush off the question.

"Honestly, no," I admitted, my voice barely above a whisper. "It's been a tough day."

Kelli patted the bed beside her, and I sank down, grateful for her presence. As I shared some of what I was feeling, her eyes softened with understanding.

"You're not alone, Claire," she said firmly. "We all feel that way sometimes. But you've got this, I believe in you."

This is my reason. This is why God has put me here. God has provided me with people like Kelli, and my mother. Which is all I could ever ask for at a big peak in my stress as I am entering college, especially at a big university like UNC.

 Pretty late that night, I knelt by my bed, the room bathed in the soft glow of Kelli's fairy lights. My prayer wasn't eloquent or long; it was raw and honest. "Lord, I'm scared. I don't know if I can do this, but I know You've brought me here for a reason. Please give me the strength to keep going. Help me to trust in Your plan and lean on the people You've placed in my life."

 As I spoke the words, I felt a sense of calm wash over me, a reminder that *I wasn't carrying this burden alone.*

6

Nurse-aid had a substitute today, and every day we had one, we were supposed to admit to the library.

As I buried myself in a sea of anatomy textbooks at the library, the last person I expected to see was Sutton, especially not with that unmistakable smirk on his face.

He spotted the stack of anatomy textbooks on my table and couldn't resist teasing me. "Still fine, huh?"

I sighed, refusing to look up, but my face burned with a mix of irritation and something I couldn't quite place. Why did he always have this effect on me?

Part of me wanted to snap back with a sharp retort, but the other part, the one that felt the weight of my own struggles, wanted to crumple under the pressure.

I hated how he always seemed to see right through me, how his words, even in jest, left cracks in the armor I worked so hard to maintain.

"Yes, Sutton, still fine."

"You know," he said, plopping into the chair across from me, "I've got a solid A+ in that class. I could tutor you."

I rolled my eyes. "Thanks, but no thanks."

I felt a nudge in my spirit as I sat on my soft comforter in the dorm, like God was saying,

"Why are you so resistant to help?"

It was a humbling thought, but I wasn't ready to act on it just yet.

As I sat there, staring at my books, I couldn't shake the feeling of being seen, really seen, by Sutton. He always had this infuriating ability to get under my skin, to pull apart the walls I'd carefully built around myself. It wasn't just the teasing. It was the way he looked at me, like he could see the cracks in my armor and wasn't afraid to point them out. But when he offered to help, it wasn't just teasing anymore.

There was something deeper in his tone, something I wasn't ready to acknowledge. It felt too close, too vulnerable. Accepting his help would mean admitting that I wasn't as in control as I wanted to be, and that was something I wasn't sure I could do.

When Sutton leaned forward, his voice softened, the teasing edge replaced with something I wasn't expecting.

"I'm serious, Claire. I can help. You don't have to do this on your own."

His words hung in the air between us, and for a moment, I saw a flicker of sincerity in his eyes. It was disarming.

The shift in his tone, gentler, almost earnest. It made me freeze for a moment, my pen hovering over the notebook. I looked up, meeting his eyes, and for the first time, I didn't see the confident quarterback who always seemed to have the upper hand.

I saw something else. Concern? Vulnerability?

I couldn't quite place it, but it made my chest tighten in a way I wasn't prepared for. I felt heat rising to my cheeks, but I refused to let him win that easily.

"You're shameless, you know that?"

As I said that, with no hesitation did Sutton respond, "Do you doubt me? He leaned back, a victorious smirk spreading across his face.

"Hey, if it gets me a seat at your table, I'll take the title"

Woah.

When I heard those words roll of his tongue, my body got sudden cold chills. I tried to hide the smile glaring across my face, ear to hear. So I looked down.

Hold it together, Claire. He doesn't mean what he says.

I couldnt help but think.

As I decided to look back up, I answered with, "You really think you can help me?" My voice softer than I intended.

"Yeah," he said, his gaze steady. "I do." It was disarming, and I felt off balance.

I hated how much it affected me. I wanted to argue, to push him away like I always did, but something in his expression stopped me. I didn't know how to respond, so I deflected with a half-hearted shrug.

"I've got it under control," I muttered, though we both knew it was a lie.

Sutton's offer stung a little; admitting I wasn't perfect felt like I'd failed. But as I watched him lean back in his chair, that cocky smirk softening just a little, I found myself wondering: what if he wasn't just mocking me? What if he really wanted to help? Sutton wasn't who he used to be, at least, not entirely. The boy I'd spent years arguing with, the one who always seemed to have a witty comeback, now seemed genuinely concerned. I wasn't sure if I could trust it, but the sincerity in his eyes made me pause. But maybe it was more about learning to trust, not just in him, but in God's timing.

As much as I hated to admit it, Sutton's offer wasn't just a kindness; it was a chance to bridge the gap between us, a way for him to prove himself as something more than just the quarterback who'd mocked me. I'd have to be vulnerable to allow that. The next morning, I sat at my desk in anatomy, still replaying Sutton's offer in my mind. Could I really let him help me? Could I accept the fact that I wasn't perfect, that I needed assistance?

My anatomy teacher substitute was talking to us in the library, and it was going in one ear, and out the other. My mind seemed to understand one word that caught my attention.

Project.

As that word was said, my whole body was given chills, whether it was the thought of the project I had worked on my junior year of high-school with Sutton, or the fact I heard the words,

"This may take a couple weeks to complete, but will be a major part of you all's grade. Good luck!"

And on that note, it came into realization. I was given a Nurse-Aid project. *This is exactly what I need as an end of the semester project.* I remember thinking to myself. After a couple of minutes just wandering around, I decided I wanted to focus on how to provide care for a patient recovering from surgery. The assignment required me to create a care plan that covered everything from monitoring the patient's physical health to offering emotional support during their recovery.

Since I had always been drawn to the idea of helping people heal, I felt like this would be the perfect opportunity to apply both my knowledge and my compassion. I started by researching common post-surgical complications, particularly focusing on things like infection prevention, pain management, and promoting mobility. I learned how crucial it was to monitor vital signs regularly and keep a close eye on wound care, ensuring the patient didn't develop any infections or complications. I spent hours in the library, and while I felt productive, there was also a nagging feeling in the back of my mind that I wasn't doing enough. I could tell that this project was going to require more than just textbook knowledge, it was going to need a piece of my heart.

As much as I loved nursing, the thought of facing real patients in the future terrified me. How would I handle the responsibility? Could I really handle the emotional strain that came with seeing people in pain, needing my help? The day went on, and the thought of Sutton tutoring me made me uneasy, but there was also something oddly comforting about it. Maybe it wasn't such a bad idea. The library was quieter than usual that day, and I could still hear Sutton's teasing tone echoing in my head. "Still fine, huh?" His smile had been full of playful confidence, but there was something different in his eyes when he said it.

He wasn't just teasing me; he was offering something genuine, something I hadn't expected from him. It wasn't just about academics. It felt like a step toward something bigger.

As I reached for my pen, Sutton's hand brushed mine, and I *FROZE.*

It was barely a touch, just the briefest graze of skin, but it sent an unexpected jolt through me. He didn't pull away immediately, his fingers lingering just a second too long, and when I finally glanced up, he was watching me with an expression I couldn't quite read.

"Relax," he said, his voice laced with humor but softer than before. "It's not like I bite."

I let out a breath I didn't realize I'd been holding, my eyes flicking to his hand resting casually on the table. How did he manage to walk the line between infuriating and strangely comforting?

"You're awfully confident for someone who barely knows me,"

 I said, trying to inject some sarcasm into my tone, though it came out weaker than I'd hoped.

 Sutton chuckled, leaning just a fraction closer.

"Oh, I think I know you better than you think. You act like you've got it all together, but I see you, Claire. You care too much, and you carry it all on your shoulders because you're scared to let anyone else in."

My breath caught, and I hated how his words struck a nerve I hadn't expected. I looked away, trying to collect myself, but the truth of his statement hung between us, heavy and unspoken. My hand trembled slightly as I withdrew, and I hated that he'd noticed.

 "I wouldn't be so sure," I shot back, hoping my sarcasm would mask the way my heart was racing.

My stomach flipped to the edge in his tone, and I quickly turned my attention back to my notes, pretending not to notice the heat rising in my cheeks. Sutton chuckled under his breath, clearly pleased with himself, and I had to fight the urge to throw my pen at him. He was infuriating. But somehow, that made him all the more captivating.

As Sutton stood to leave, he glanced back over his shoulder, his grin as infuriating as ever.

"Don't think too hard about it, Claire. You might hurt yourself."

I threw a crumpled piece of paper at him, and he caught it effortlessly, laughing as he did.

"You're impossible," I muttered, but the corners of my mouth betrayed me, twitching upward despite myself.

He took a step closer, leaning down until his face was level with mine. "Impossible?" he repeated, his voice soft but teasing. "Or unforgettable?"

My breath caught in my lungs. Before I could come up a clever retort, Sutton leaned in close to my face.

"Can I walk you back to your dorm?" He asked.

Shock shot through me, but I felt myself nodding yes without hesitation.

As we walked to the door of the library, the silence between us was charged with an energy I couldn't quite explain. He held the door open for me, his hand brushing mine once again as I passed. The touch was fleeting, but it sent a spark through me, and I found myself glancing up at him. He watched me with that same infuriatingly confident grin, but there was something deeper in his eyes, something that made my breath hitch.

"You're thinking too hard again," he said softly, his tone gentler now. "What's on your mind?"

I shook my head, trying to shake off the way his presence seemed to unravel my carefully built walls.

"Nothing," I lied.

He didn't push, but the way his gaze lingered on mine told me he didn't believe me.

"Well," he said after a moment, his voice light but with a teasing edge, "if you ever decide to stop overthinking everything, let me know. I'll be here. Have a good rest of your afternoon, Claire."

And with that, he turned and walked away, leaving me standing there, my heart pounding and my thoughts spinning. In my dorm room, Kelli sat on her bed flipping through a magazine. The door clicked shut behind me, and I sighed as I dropped my bag to the floor. I couldn't stop thinking about Sutton. Why had he offered to tutor me? Was it because he really wanted to help, or was there some other motive I wasn't seeing? It was easy for me to assume he was just being nice for the sake of his own pride, but deep down, I felt like there was something genuine in his offer. Maybe he was tired of the way things had been between us. Maybe he was trying to show that he had changed, that he wasn't the same person who once teased me without a second thought. But the question lingered,

Did I need his help? Could I let him in after all this time?

My mind kept going back and forth, torn between the practical side of me that wanted to say no and the side of me that was beginning to wonder if I could trust him. The thought of vulnerability still unsettled me, but there was something in his eyes that made me pause. Maybe it wasn't just about anatomy. Maybe it was a bigger step forward for both of us. I thought back to the first time I met Sutton.

I still remember how he looked that day: tall and broad-shouldered, his brunette hair slightly tousled from practice. His eyes, a piercing blue, seemed to always carry a challenge, as if daring you to question him. He had that confidence about him, the kind of attitude that made him stand out even without trying. But even though everyone else admired him, I always felt like there was a wall between us, built out of all the snide comments and jokes he made. We'd argue so many times over the years,mostly about things that didn't matter, but there was always something underlying those arguments. It was like we couldn't just be normal around each other.

Every time we had a confrontation, it felt like there was more at stake than just the words we were saying.

I couldn't help but wonder if it was always that way because of the tension, the differences in our worlds, he, the star quarterback, and me, just trying to make it through college without standing out too much. I'd seen him laugh with his teammates, joke around with friends, and I'd always been on the outside looking in. He didn't know what it was like to struggle like I did.

But I also couldn't deny that when we talked, really talked, it felt different. There were moments when his usual bravado would fade, and I'd catch glimpses of something more real behind his confident exterior.

And now, here he was, offering to help me.

The guy who'd been at the center of every embarrassing moment I'd faced, the one who seemed to always make me feel *small* in comparison.

It wasn't easy to reconcile that with the guy who was now offering me his help, who was trying to be something more than the person I had built up in my mind.

As I sat there thinking about Sutton, I noticed my heart rate picking up. He was a complicated person, and I had always tried to keep my distance from him, mainly because it was easier than letting him in. But now, I couldn't shake the thought that maybe, just maybe, there was a chance for something different between us. A chance to not just fight, but to understand each other.

"Long day?" Kelli asked, pulling me back into the moment as I stood at the door.

"Yeah, I ran into Sutton at the library."

Her head whipped up immediately, her eyebrows raised in curiosity. "Sutton? As in the quarterback?"

"Yeah," I said, sinking into my chair. "He offered to tutor me in anatomy."

Kelli's lips parted in surprise. "Wait, what? The guy who used to joke about you not being able to understand the class?"

"Yeah," I replied, feeling a little embarrassed. "I was so resistant to his help. But I think it's more than just a tutoring thing. I think he's trying to make up for… well, everything."

Kelli nodded thoughtfully. "Sounds like he's trying to show you that he's changed. That's big, Claire."

I sat back, still processing everything. "I don't know if I'm ready to let him in like that, though."

"Well, you don't have to let him in all at once," Kelli said, smiling softly. "Just take it one step at a time."

We sat in silence for a few moments, and I felt the weight of my decision. I had to decide if I was ready to trust Sutton, if I could let go of my pride and accept his offer.

The thought of it still made me feel vulnerable, but maybe that was what I needed. Later, as I studied for another class, I couldn't help but think about how I was doing in the rest of my courses. The biology exam coming up was starting to feel like a mountain I didn't know how to climb. But I was staying on top of things in my other classes.

Psychology was going better than I had expected, and I was finding history to be surprisingly interesting this semester. It was just anatomy that had me stuck, the one class I felt like I could never quite catch up with.

Despite the progress I was making in other areas, the thought of asking Sutton for help still hung in the back of my mind. I wasn't sure I could bring myself to take him up on his offer, but the more I thought about it, the more it seemed like the right thing to do. If I could just let go of my pride, if I could be humble enough to ask for help, maybe I'd be stronger for it in the end. Maybe it would be the start of something new, not just for me, but for my friendship with Sutton too.

Later that night, I sat on my bed and prayed, seeking peace. "God, I know I'm on the right path. I feel it in my soul, but why does it feel so overwhelming sometimes? Please help me find the courage to trust in myself and in you. I can't do this alone."

I continued developing the care plan, but the pressure was starting to get to me. It felt like there was so much to consider. On top of the usual college stress, I had to figure out how to balance my emotions with being a source of strength for someone else. That morning, as I was getting dressed for class, I noticed the way I looked in the mirror.

I'd been feeling this growing discontent with my appearance lately, which felt so superficial but also impossible to ignore. I didn't look like the polished, put-together girls in the halls of my dorm. I had a few extra pounds, my hair didn't fall perfectly, and my skin wasn't clear, things I felt I had to keep under control, especially with all the people around me who seemed so effortlessly perfect. I hated feeling like I wasn't enough.

I prayed silently, "God, I don't want to keep thinking this way. I feel like I'm always trying to meet some standard that's not even mine. Help me see myself the way you do."

It was hard not to compare myself to others. I watched girls like Kelli, who always looked flawless, confident and at ease in her own skin. She had that kind of effortless charm that made everything look easy. Meanwhile, I was stuck in this cycle of self-criticism, worried about my body image.

I often felt like I was the last person in the room people would pay attention to, and that insecurity seeped into everything else. Would I even be a good nurse if I didn't have that self-assurance?

I sat in the library again, my head buried in books, trying to focus on patient care but unable to push the feelings aside. I hadn't told anyone about how self-conscious I felt, not even Kelli. It was like I was trapped in my own mind, feeling embarrassed by how much I was letting it affect me. I couldn't understand. Out of all honesty, my distractions had got to me, and I did not want in the last way to be honest with myself and agree. I had been scrolling Instagram in my free time, and my worse-half had gotten to me. How could I help Kelli if she is struggling?

Or what if God puts me in a situation Im not sure if I can do? After all, how could I be a source of support for someone else if I couldn't even support myself? I paused for a moment, staring at my anatomy textbook. The words blurred together, and I realized I was letting the stress overwhelm me. I turned to my phone and sent a quick message to God, as silly as it might sound. "Please, God, help me find peace with who I am. I can't keep feeling this way. I want to be confident and not let my appearance control me." The thought of my insecurity felt like a weight on my chest. It wasn't just about the way I looked; it was deeper. I constantly doubted myself, worried that I wasn't worthy or good enough, and these thoughts came creeping in, making it even harder to focus on things that mattered. But I kept pushing forward, telling myself I couldn't let these doubts define me. I spent another few hours that day refining my care plan.

I'd gone through every detail, ensuring I wasn't missing anything, how to manage pain, how to track changes in the patient's vitals, and how to provide emotional support. But the deeper I got into the project, the more I realized that it wasn't just about checking off tasks, it was about making a real, tangible difference in someone's life. That thought hit me harder than I expected. Could I really be the one to give this kind of care? It felt overwhelming. But there was something inside me that whispered, Yes, you can. You're capable of more than you think.

As I stared at my textbooks, a quiet voice whispered in my heart: "*Trust the process*."

As I sat there, the weight of the decision pressing on my chest, I couldn't help but think about all the times I had pushed people away in an effort to protect myself. I had built walls around my heart to keep from getting hurt, to keep from being vulnerable.

But now, with Sutton's offer hanging in the air, I realized that maybe I was missing out on something more valuable, something deeper. My pride had always been my shield, but perhaps it was time to let it down and trust that God had a plan for me, even in moments like this. Sutton's kindness, though it still made me uncomfortable, was an opportunity to grow, both academically and personally.

Kelli's words echoed in my mind: "Just take it one step at a time."

It was simple, but it felt like the wisdom I needed to hear. Maybe the first step was just acknowledging that I didn't have to do it all alone. Maybe I could accept Sutton's help without losing myself in the process. The more I thought about it, the more it felt like the right choice, not just for my grades, but for the potential it had to change the dynamics between us.

Maybe, just maybe, Sutton was offering me the chance to see him as more than the person I had always resented. I wasn't ready to make any promises, but the thought of it stirred something inside me.

The following night, I had ANOTHER conversation with God: "God, I know you're leading me toward this. But I'm scared. What if I can't do it? What if I fail? Please, give me the strength to keep moving forward, even when I'm not sure of myself."

I was sitting in the library again, working on refining the role-playing part of my project. I practiced how I would approach a patient, how I would communicate with both the patient and their family, and how I would approach delicate topics like pain management or asking for help.

But as I was practicing my script, I couldn't help but feel like I was still pretending. I wasn't truly believing in my ability to carry this out.

I was worried I'd fail the project, and worse, I was worried I'd fail at being the person I wanted to be. I had been so focused on the care plan, but I hadn't truly considered how much it would take out of me emotionally to provide that care.

In my reflection, I asked God, "Lord, how can I be a nurse if I can't even trust in myself? I don't want to pretend anymore, but I feel so lost. I need your help to see my worth and to be strong in moments when I feel weak."

That afternoon, Sutton found me again in the library. He always had a way of appearing at the most inconvenient times, like when I was deep in thought or stressed out. But this time, something in me shifted.

When he saw me with my anatomy book, he didn't tease me. Instead, he asked me how I was doing. I appreciated it more than I could say. I felt vulnerable, still dealing with my own internal struggles, but Sutton's sincerity was like a small flicker of light in the middle of my chaos.

"I'm just... not sure I can do this," I said quietly, tapping the edge of my book.

"It feels like everything is riding on me, and I'm not sure I'm good enough."

He raised an eyebrow and gave me a soft, almost serious smile. "You are enough, Claire," he said. "You've always been enough. And you don't have to do it all by yourself."

That simple encouragement was like a breath of fresh air. I didn't know if I fully believed it yet, but maybe, just maybe, it was enough to keep moving forward. I was back at my desk, finishing the final touches on my project. I still wasn't completely confident in myself, but I had come to realize that I didn't have to be perfect. I didn't have to have everything figured out right now. The important thing was that I was trying. I was learning to embrace the process, to give myself grace, and to trust that the small steps I was taking would lead me to where I needed to be.

Before submitting the project, I had another conversation with God: "God, I'm still scared, but I trust that You've got a plan. Thank you for being with me through this. I'm learning to trust in myself and in You. Please help me to keep moving forward with faith."

After weeks of hard work, I finally hit that submit button, and a wave of relief washed over me. The weight of the project had been heavy, constantly pulling at me, but now it was over. I couldn't help but feel a mix of exhaustion and satisfaction. I had put so much into it, research, planning, emotional energy, and now I could take a breath. I leaned back in my chair, letting out a sigh of relief. "It's done. I actually did it," I whispered to myself, a smile slowly spreading across my face. I had doubted myself so many times throughout the process, but now, looking back, I realized how much I'd grown.

Not just in my knowledge, but in my ability to trust myself and push through fear. I felt lighter, like I had been carrying a burden for too long, and now I was finally free. There was a calmness in knowing I had done my best and, no matter what, that was enough. The project was submitted, and I felt a weight lift off my shoulders. It wasn't perfect, but I had done my best. Through this project, I learned more about myself than I expected. I learned that being vulnerable was part of being strong, and that real growth didn't come from having everything figured out, it came from taking one step at a time and trusting God with the rest.

My appearance, my fears, my self-doubt... they didn't define me. I was still learning to believe that, but I was getting closer every day.I closed my anatomy book, my mind still racing. I wasn't sure if I was ready to reach out to Sutton yet, but the seed had been planted. And sometimes, that's all it takes. A small step forward, even when you don't know exactly where it's going to lead. I could trust that God would guide me through this, just as He *always* had.

7

The third time Sutton offered to tutor me, I was desperate enough to say yes. We met in the library, and to my surprise, he was actually… good at it. He had a way of breaking down complex concepts that made them click.

"You're not as dumb as you look," I teased after a particularly productive session.

"High praise coming from you," he shot back with a grin.

Our sessions started out awkward, both of us fumbling through the material in silence at first, but soon, Sutton's natural knack for teaching began to shine through. One evening, as we studied the intricacies of cellular respiration, Sutton explained how the electron transport chain worked in a way that finally made sense.

"Think of it like a factory assembly line," he said. "The electrons are the raw materials, and the proteins act as the workers who transfer them through the chain. By the end, you've created ATP, like the finished product that powers the entire cell."

I looked at him, wide-eyed. "That actually makes sense!"

He grinned, his usual cocky smile softening into something more genuine. "I'm just getting started," he teased, sliding his notes over to me.

Another time, we were reviewing the skeletal system, and Sutton went the extra mile.

He brought a model to help me visualize the bones better. "This is your humerus," he said, holding up the model. "The name sounds funny, but it's the bone that gives you your upper arm strength. Let's take a look at how the muscles and tendons connect to it."

Sutton patiently explained the differences between ligaments and tendons, pointing to the model as he did.

As I practiced labeling the bones, Sutton held out a small, red pen and tapped the bones I missed, offering encouraging words when I got it right. "There you go. That's it!" he'd say, his voice brimming with excitement.

Our study sessions became something I looked forward to. Sutton was focused and driven, and I started to see a side of him I hadn't noticed before.

He wasn't just the quarterback with a reputation to uphold, he was a guy with patience, a desire to help, and a surprising level of care for something he didn't have to care about.

After each session, I prayed with a heart full of gratitude. "Lord, thank You for using Sutton to help me. And thank You for showing me that people can change."

Our connection grew deeper during those hours. Every time I saw Sutton's dedication to helping me, I realized how much more he had to offer beyond the surface.

The confidence he exuded in his studies was slowly changing the way I saw him, and maybe, just maybe, I was starting to see him as someone who had more potential than I ever gave him credit for. The sessions with Sutton continued to transform my understanding of the material. One afternoon, as we sat across from each other in the library, I realized I had finally grasped the concept of mitosis.

"Okay, so this is when the cell divides, right? I remember that it has these stages, prophase, metaphase, anaphase, and telophase," I said, confident in my explanation.

Sutton leaned back in his chair, a proud grin stretching across his face. "That's exactly it. You're really starting to get the hang of this."

He picked up a piece of paper and drew a quick diagram, tracing the phases of mitosis in sharp, deliberate strokes. "This diagram might help solidify it even more," he said, pushing the paper toward me. I stared at the diagram, feeling a spark of excitement.

"You're a good teacher, Sutton," I said, surprised by how much I was starting to enjoy these sessions.

Sutton gave me a cocky wink, but I could see the hint of pride in his eyes.

With each passing day, I began to feel more confident in my abilities, but it wasn't just the material that was changing. It was the way I saw Sutton.

The old, cocky quarterback was still there, but beneath that layer, I could sense a level of depth I hadn't noticed before. He was patient with me, and that patience began to show through in the way he interacted with others as well.

He was evolving, and I was beginning to feel like I was evolving with him.

The physical signs of his encouragement were there too, whenever I got something right, Sutton's face would light up. His eyebrows would lift, and his eyes would soften in a way that made me feel like I had accomplished something significant. Sometimes, he'd even give me a fist bump or a high five.

 Other times, he'd let out a small laugh and say, "See? I knew you could do it."

There were moments when the two of us would be buried in notes, completely immersed in our work, but there was a growing comfort between us.

Every time I got something right, Sutton's eyes softened as if he wasn't just proud of my progress, but of me as a person. His gaze held something more, a quiet affection I couldn't quite understand but felt deeply. We'd talk about everything, his football games, my classes, our families, even our favorite movies. I wasn't sure if it was just the studying or if it was something more, but spending time with Sutton started to feel like the highlight of my day.

That evening, as I knelt beside my bed, I paused, my hands clasped together in prayer. "Lord, thank You for helping me understand these subjects. Thank You for letting Sutton be the one to show me how to learn. I've seen his heart change, and I'm so grateful. But I don't know if this is all a sign. Is this You working through him? Is it a sign of something bigger? Please, Lord, show me if I'm on the right path."

I closed my eyes and silently waited for a sense of peace or a sign, but all I heard was the quiet hum of my dorm room.

A faint breeze fluttered through the window. I didn't get an immediate answer, but something in my heart told me that maybe I didn't need to know everything right away. The next time I saw Sutton in the library, he was focused, but there was a tenderness in his manner that made me pause. I had never noticed how his eyes softened when he talked about his younger sister or how much care he took with the smallest details of our study sessions. It was as if he wasn't just teaching me science; he was teaching me about life in his own quiet way.

And the more I understood, the more I started to see that my prayers might be working.

The sessions continued, each one bringing us closer, and with each meeting, I realized that learning wasn't just about textbooks and notes, it was about connecting with the person teaching you, letting the lessons become a shared experience. Sutton had gone from being a guy I barely knew to someone I trusted deeply.

And for the first time in a long time, I felt like I wasn't alone in my studies, or in life.

As the days passed, our sessions became even more comfortable. I began to notice that Sutton wasn't just a tutor anymore; he was becoming a friend.

The laughter between us came more easily, the tension from our earlier awkward moments slowly fading away.

One afternoon, as we struggled through a particularly tricky section on enzyme functions, Sutton made a joke about how our brains must be like enzymes, slowly catalyzing our way through the material.

I laughed out loud, nearly snorting in the process, which made Sutton burst into laughter too. "Did you really just snort?" he asked, a grin slid across his face.

"Shut up," I laughed, trying to hide my embarrassment, but I couldn't stop smiling.

His laugh was contagious, and before I knew it, we were both doubled over in laughter.

The tension that had once filled the room was now replaced by the sound of our shared amusement.

"Okay, okay, I'll stop making fun of you," Sutton said, wiping tears from his eyes. "But seriously, you're getting this. I can tell."

I shook my head, still laughing.

"I think you're just happy you got me to laugh at something other than my mistakes."

He shrugged with a grin, his eyes sparkling. "I can't help it. You make studying fun, you know?"

His words hung in the air, and for a moment, I felt something shift between us.

When we laughed together, it wasn't just the joke that filled the room. It was the comfort of knowing that, in that moment, we didn't need to pretend.

We were simply two people finding joy in each other's company. We weren't just two people who had been paired together for the sake of academics. There was a deeper connection forming, one that went beyond the textbooks. It wasn't just about learning anymore; it was about enjoying each other's company.

As the weeks wore on, I couldn't help but notice how quickly Thanksgiving was approaching. The semester had flown by, and the weather had shifted from the warmth of early fall to the crisp chill of late November. One afternoon, as we wrapped up another successful study session, I looked up at the clock and realized how close the holiday was.

"Can you believe Thanksgiving is next week?" I asked, leaning back in my chair. "It feels like this semester has just flown by."

Sutton leaned against the table, stretching his arms above his head. "I know, right? It's been crazy." Sutton's expression softened as he looked at me, his gaze turning serious for a moment.

"Hey, I've been meaning to say something," he started, his voice quieter than usual.

"I'm sorry for what I said back in high school. I was an idiot, and I know I hurt you. I wasn't thinking clearly." He paused, his eyes filled with sincerity. "And I'm sorry for anything I ever did that brought drama or chaos into your life. You didn't deserve that."

His words caught me off guard, but they also meant more to me than I could put into words. It was like a weight had been lifted, and in that moment, I realized just how much he had changed.

When an unexpected apology came out of Sutton Adams mouth, I felt something deep within me, an unspoken healing that started to mend the wounds I had carried for so long.

And in that moment, I realized that the road we were on wasn't just about academics or friendship, it was about redemption, about second chances.

And then a thought crossed my mind, and before I could stop myself, I blurted it out. "What are you thankful for, Sutton?" I asked, curious.

He raised an eyebrow, clearly surprised by the question. "Huh. I guess I've never really thought about it. I mean, I'm thankful for my family, football, and stuff like that. But I guess lately, I've been thankful for... well, these study sessions. And for you, actually."

I blinked, a little caught off guard by his honesty. "Me?" I asked, feeling my cheeks heat up.

He nodded, looking serious for a moment before his usual playful grin returned. "Yeah, you. You've made this whole semester a lot better, and not just because you're finally getting the material. I don't know, I guess it's just been nice to have someone to talk to, you know?"

I felt my heart warm at his words. I wasn't sure if I had ever heard him say something quite that genuine. It made me realize just how much our friendship had grown over the past few weeks.

"I'm thankful for you too," I said quietly, smiling up at him. "For everything."

There was a moment of silence as we both absorbed the weight of what had just been said. Then, to break the tension, I added, "Okay, enough of this stuff. Let's get back to these enzymes, shall we?"

Sutton laughed again, his usual cocky charm returning. "Alright, alright. But seriously, you're doing great. We've got this."

There was a quiet understanding between us now, a wordless exchange that spoke volumes.

When Sutton handed me my notes, I realized that the academic barrier between us had dissolved. What was left was simply us, two people navigating life and learning together. Sutton's voice was different now, like it held more weight.

Every time he praised me or pushed me to do better, I felt something shift inside. It wasn't just his belief in me, it was his belief in us, in the way we were growing, side by side.

As I sat there, feeling a mix of gratitude and peace, I realized just how much I had to be thankful for. Not only had I learned more about cellular respiration, enzymes, and the skeletal system, but I had also learned a lot about myself, and about Sutton. The fact that he was thankful for me, in his own way, felt like an answered prayer, a sign that my faith and my prayers were being heard.

I remember thinking, *Sutton didn't just help me with my grades; he helped me with my fears, my doubts. When he told me I could do this, he wasn't just talking about enzymes or cellular respiration, he was talking about life, and for the first time, I believed him.*

And that brought me peace, I never would have imagined. The peace that settled over me wasn't just because of the prayers I'd said or the progress I'd made in my studies. It was the realization that, in this journey of growth, I wasn't alone. Sutton had become someone who saw me, someone who accepted me, not just for my strengths, but for my weaknesses, too.

As I packed up my things that evening, my thoughts swirled with everything that had changed over the past few months. What had started as a simple offer for help had transformed into something I hadn't expected, something deeper.

Sutton and I had gone from strangers to study partners, then friends, and now, it seemed like we were both finding new parts of ourselves through each other.

The lessons I had learned weren't just from anatomy and biology; they were about trust, about letting someone in, about giving people the chance to change. Sutton wasn't the same person I had resented in high school. He had evolved, and in a way, so had I. I felt a quiet gratitude for how much I had grown, not just in my knowledge of the human body, but in the way I viewed others, especially Sutton.

As I walked back to my dorm, I felt the crisp November air against my skin, and for the first time in a long while, I felt peaceful. The tension I had carried for so long was finally starting to melt away, and it was replaced by a sense of calm and hope. I wasn't sure what the future held, but I knew one thing: I wasn't facing it alone.

Whether it was in my studies, in my relationships, or in my faith, I was learning that being vulnerable didn't make me weak, it made me stronger. And sometimes, God uses the most unexpected people and situations to show us that. Sutton's apology, his genuine words of gratitude, had been a turning point. I could see the sincerity in his eyes, and it made me realize just how much we had both changed.

There was a healing that took place in that moment, a healing that had been long overdue. For the first time, I saw Sutton not as the guy who used to make fun of me, but as someone who cared, someone who had grown into a man who understood the value of kindness and humility. I didn't know exactly what was going to happen between us, but I knew that I was grateful for the journey we had shared so far.

As I knelt beside my bed that night, the soft glow of the lamp casting gentle shadows across my room, I prayed again. "Thank You, Lord, for bringing Sutton into my life in this way. Thank You for showing me how to open my heart, to trust, and to see the good in others. I'm learning so much, and I know You're guiding me through it. Please help me continue to be open to Your plan, even when I don't understand it fully."

I paused, feeling the stillness of the moment wash over me. It wasn't about having all the answers. It was about knowing that God was with me every step of the way, guiding me through the moments of doubt and uncertainty, and reminding me that growth comes from the most unexpected places.

I closed my eyes, feeling a deep sense of peace settle in my chest. It wasn't just about Thanksgiving anymore. It was about the gratitude I felt for the transformation that had taken place in me, and in Sutton, and in our connection. This chapter of my life wasn't just about studying; it was about finding trust, healing, and a deeper understanding of what it meant to love and support one another. Just the thought of Sutton Adams made my stomach turn. I had never felt this kind of affection towards a guy, besides God, and my father. I just couldnt understand.

Everything Sutton did, I felt like I had to get involved. Like I had to be there. Like I was his supervisor. I could not understand it.

But I knew I was in his life for a reason, and God put him in mine for a *reason*.

8

I woke up to the soft light of Thanksgiving morning streaming through my window, the warmth of the sun gently kissing my skin.

The air outside was crisp, and there was a sense of peace that filled my heart. I lay in bed for a moment, reflecting on all the blessings in my life. The soft hum of the world waking up around me reminded me that I had so much to be thankful for. I thought of my family, my friends, the opportunities I had to learn and grow, and the love I felt from those around me.

Most of all, I was thankful for my faith.

The way it grounded me and gave me a sense of purpose. It was through my faith that I found peace in even the most chaotic moments, and it was through prayer that I found the courage to face each day. I smiled to myself, knowing that my heart was full of gratitude for so many things, even the little moments that often went unnoticed.

As I made my way downstairs for breakfast, I thought about what Sutton had said a couple of days ago when we were talking about Thanksgiving.

"I mean, I'm thankful for my family, football, and stuff like that. But I guess lately, I've been thankful for... well, these study sessions. And for YOU, actually."

His words had taken me by surprise, catching me off guard. It was clear that he was struggling to express his gratitude, and yet there was something so sincere about it. I could see that, despite his casual tone, Sutton was opening up in his own way, acknowledging the small things that had begun to matter more to him lately.

There was a vulnerability in the way he spoke, as if he was slowly starting to recognize that there was more to life than what he had been focusing on for so long. His words stayed with me, echoing in my mind. I could tell that he was struggling with something deeper, something that he hadn't fully come to terms with yet. It made me wonder if he realized that what he was searching for could be found in God, the peace, the purpose, the sense of belonging that only a relationship with Him could provide. Sutton had always been a bit distant when it came to matters of faith, but I could see in his eyes that there was a longing there, something he couldn't quite articulate but felt nonetheless. Sutton had always been a strong figure, both physically and mentally.

As a football player, he had the discipline and focus that came with the sport. The way he approached each game, each practice, was a reflection of his commitment. It wasn't just about winning or being the best on the field, it was about pushing his limits, about showing up for his team, and about finding the strength to keep going even when things seemed tough.

But beyond that, there were moments when he seemed almost exhausted, like the weight of everything was starting to pull him down. I couldn't help but wonder if the pressure of football, his future, and the expectations he placed on himself were beginning to take a toll on him.

I knew that Sutton had dreams of becoming a doctor, and I admired that.

His ambition was one of the things that made him so driven, so focused. But sometimes, I wondered if he was putting so much energy into his future that he was losing sight of the present, of the things that truly mattered, like his mental well-being, his sense of peace, and his relationship with God.

It was hard to tell whether Sutton's mind was at peace or if he was carrying around more than he could handle. Between his demanding schedule with football and his academic goals, I could sense that there was a quiet struggle inside him, one that he didn't always express. Sutton's desire to become a doctor showed that he had a heart for helping others, and I believed that part of his struggle came from trying to figure out how to balance his ambitions with his emotional health.

Sometimes, it felt like he was constantly chasing something, success, perfection, approval, and yet I could see the moments where he just seemed worn out, as if he couldn't keep up with everything at once. I prayed that he would realize that in the pursuit of all these things, he didn't have to do it alone.

There was a peace and rest that came from knowing that God was always there, ready to carry the weight of our burdens if we were willing to trust Him. I knew that Sutton's relationship with God wasn't where it needed to be. He had grown up in a world that didn't place much emphasis on faith, and for him, religion seemed more like a distant concept than something that could truly change his life. But I also knew that God was working in his heart, just as He was in mine. I believed that there was a longing deep within Sutton, a desire to find something more, something that could give his life meaning.

But how could I help him see that?

How could I show him the beauty of a relationship with God, and how that relationship could transform everything?

I prayed for him often, asking God to open his heart and guide him toward the truth. I knew that it wouldn't be an easy journey for Sutton, but I also knew that God had a plan for him. I didn't know when or how it would happen, but I trusted that God was planting seeds in his heart, just as He had in mine. It was my hope and my prayer that one day, Sutton would see the beauty of faith and come to experience the joy and peace that I had found in my relationship with God.

And right then, on that Thanksgiving morning, I realized that it was time to take another step. Maybe it wasn't about trying to fix everything or have all the answers.

Maybe it was simply about offering Sutton the opportunity to experience God's love in a way that felt real to him.

I took a deep breath and said a quiet prayer: "Lord, help me to be a light for Sutton. Show me how to love him in a way that draws him closer to You."

I was ready to take that leap of faith.

As I drove home from the University of North Carolina to Chapel Hill, the familiarity of the road brought me a sense of comfort.

The trees, bare in the early winter chill, lined the highway in quiet rows, and the small towns I passed through had a peaceful, almost nostalgic quality to them. I marveled at how far I had come, both physically and emotionally.

There was a time when the thought of driving alone would have filled me with fear, but now, the open road felt like a symbol of the growth I had experienced. I remembered how scared I used to be, especially when I was in high school and about to get my license. I was a sophomore, ready to finally have the independence of my own car, but then came the tragedy that shook everything.

My mom's sister, my aunt, had been in a horrific car accident, and the loss was almost unbearable. She had been taken from us too soon, and in that moment, the thought of driving felt terrifying. Every time I got behind the wheel, I saw her face in my mind's eye, and the fear would creep in, making it hard to focus on the road. It took me a long time to find the courage to drive without her memory clouding my thoughts, but eventually, I learned to lean on God's peace, trusting that He would keep me safe.

Now, as I drove down the familiar stretch of road toward home, I felt a quiet reassurance that I had finally found my way through the fear.

When I arrived home, the warmth of my family's house greeted me, and I immediately felt a sense of relief. The house smelled like turkey and pumpkin pie, and the sound of laughter floated down the hallway from the kitchen. My parents were busy preparing the meal, and my siblings were talking excitedly about their plans for the day. It was the kind of Thanksgiving I had missed, and the joy of being home made me feel deeply grateful.

I joined in the preparations, exchanging stories with my family, and for a while, everything felt perfectly right. This was home, the place where I could truly unwind and be myself. College had been a whirlwind, full of challenges and moments of self-doubt, but now, as I spent time with my family, I realized how far I had come. The stress of the first few months had been overwhelming, but it was slowly becoming manageable. I was learning to balance school, friendships, and faith, and though it wasn't always easy, I knew I was making it. Looking back, I could see how God had been guiding me through each step, even when I didn't know what was next. My heart was full, and the path ahead seemed a little clearer. After dinner, as I sat with my mom in the living room, I couldn't help but share with her how much Sutton had been helping me with my studies.

"He's been such a big help with my biology work," I said, smiling as I thought about how much he had encouraged me. "It's been great having someone to study with."

Mom raised an eyebrow and paused for a moment, clearly intrigued. "The one from your high school biology class?" she asked, her voice filled with curiosity.

I nodded, feeling a sense of warmth in my chest. "Yes, that's him. God sent him to me for a reason. I really believe that."

She smiled softly, her eyes filled with understanding. "I'm so glad to hear that. It sounds like you've found someone special to walk alongside you."

Her words brought a sense of peace to my heart, and I felt reassured that God was guiding me in all areas of my life, not just my studies. s the evening wore on, the conversation shifted to memories of past Thanksgivings, each one tinged with nostalgia and gratitude.

It was a time of reflection, and as we sat together, I realized how deeply I had missed this connection with my family. The simple joys of sharing a meal, hearing my dad's laughter echoing through the house, and the comfort of being surrounded by those who loved me, it all felt like a reminder of what truly mattered in life. My thoughts then drifted back to Sutton. I hadn't seen him since our last study session before Thanksgiving break, but I couldn't shake the feeling that something had shifted between us.

What began as a reluctant tutoring session had blossomed into a friendship, one that had started with awkwardness but now felt genuine and filled with promise.

Sutton had always been a bit of a mystery to me, strong, driven, and at times, a little closed off, but the more we studied together, the more I saw a different side to him. It was as though he was unraveling the layers that had protected him from truly connecting with others. I remembered the conversation we had about being thankful, his unexpected admission that he appreciated our study sessions and, more surprisingly, his gratitude toward me. It was a side of him I hadn't expected, and yet, in some small way, I felt like it was the beginning of something deeper.

There was a sincerity to his words, a vulnerability that he didn't often show. I had always known that Sutton had potential, the same drive that made him excel in football and academics could lead him to great things, but I wondered if he realized that success didn't always mean pushing harder and faster. Sometimes, it meant taking a step back, finding peace, and allowing God to work through the chaos.

As I sat there with my family, I realized just how much I had grown this semester, not just academically, but spiritually, emotionally, and relationally.

The time I spent with Sutton, and Kelli, the small moments of vulnerability we shared, had begun to shift something in me. I no longer saw him simply as the football star with a reputation to uphold. Instead, I saw him as someone who was still finding his way, much like I was.

I felt this gentle nudge in my heart that maybe it wasn't my role to fix everything for Sutton. Maybe it was simply about showing up for him, being a steady presence in his life, and letting God do the work. The thought of Sutton and his journey toward understanding faith kept lingering in my mind as I helped clear the table and prepared to settle into the living room for some family time. I thought back to the prayer I had whispered earlier in the morning, asking God to help me be a light for Sutton, to show him how much more there was to life than what he was chasing. It wasn't about giving him answers right away. It was about offering him a space to explore and ask questions in his own time.

I knew that God's love could soften even the hardest of hearts, and if Sutton was open to it, there was a chance for him to discover something transformative.

I sat down with my mom and dad in the living room, sipping warm tea and watching a movie, I felt a sense of peace that had settled deep into my bones. This moment, this sense of calm and belonging, was a gift that I often took for granted. My family's love, their unwavering support, was a reminder that no matter where life took me, I always had a foundation to return to. It was a reminder that no matter how far I ventured out into the world, whether through my studies, my friendships, or even the way I saw others, I would never be alone.

Later that evening, as I got ready to head back to school, I couldn't shake the feeling that something significant was happening in my life. The shifts in my relationship with Sutton, my growing sense of peace with my own faith, and the unwavering love of my family, it all felt connected in a way that only God could orchestrate. I had no idea what the future held, but I was beginning to understand that faith wasn't about having all the answers. It was about trusting God to guide you, step by step, even when the path ahead wasn't always clear. The next few months would bring new challenges, new opportunities for growth, and perhaps even new twists in my relationship with Sutton. But one thing was certain, I wasn't alone in this journey. God was with me, every step of the way. And, maybe just maybe, He was working in Sutton's heart too, slowly but surely.

With that thought, I said a quiet prayer as I grabbed my bag to leave. "Lord, help me trust You, even when the way ahead feels uncertain. And please, continue to guide Sutton, wherever his journey may lead. I know that You're always with us, and that's enough."

As I left the warmth of my family home and drove back to school campus, I realized that Thanksgiving had come to mean something even deeper than I had imagined. It was about more than just being thankful for the big things, it was about recognizing the beauty in the small moments, the moments where God's love shines through in unexpected ways. I wasn't sure what the future held for me and Sutton, but I was ready for whatever it may be, knowing that God was in control, and that His love would guide us both.

When I arrived at UNC campus, the walk upstairs to my dorm felt longer than ever. *Three more floors.* And then *two more floors.* I felt like my feet had the weight of concrete blocks. Finally, I remember thinking, *last floor Claire, almost there.*

As I opened the door from the stair case, and my dorm room was right there. I didnt shower, did not even speak to Kelli. It was dark outside, and for some reason I had never felt as tired as I did that Thanksgiving day.

When I closed my eyes that night, Sutton's face lingered in my mind, the vulnerability he'd shown at church, the way his walls had begun to crumble under the weight of grace. I hadn't thought about him in this way in so long, yet now, the feelings I had once tucked away seemed to resurface like waves after a long, quiet tide. It wasn't just about the Sutton I had known in high school, the one who made me laugh until I couldn't breathe and had a way of making everyone feel important. It was about the Sutton sitting beside me in church that morning, eyes searching, heart breaking open, desperate for something real.

That image of him stayed with me, and for the first time in years, I let myself wonder what it all meant. Sutton had always been the person people turned to in times of need, the dependable quarterback, the truly reliable friend, the steady presence on and off the field. But now, I was beginning to see that all the strength he had relied on wasn't enough to carry him through the struggles he was facing.

And maybe, just maybe, that was exactly where *God wanted him to be.*

I had never seen him like this before, raw, unguarded, and open, if only for a moment. Watching him wrestle with his doubts reminded me that faith wasn't about having all the answers. It was about stepping out in trust, even when everything felt uncertain. Sutton had spent so long trying to be enough for everyone else, but now I prayed he would see that he didn't have to be enough for God.

God was already enough for him. I remember sitting up straight, with energy that came out of nowhere. I was sittingcross-legged on my bed with my journal balanced on my knees, I couldn't help but reflect on my own journey. Seeing Sutton's struggle had stirred something inside me, a reminder of how far I had come, but also how easy it was to let doubt creep back in. Lately, with the pressure of classes, clinicals, and my future looming ahead, I had found myself slipping into old habits of self-reliance.

I told myself I was managing it all, but deep down, I knew I had been neglecting the quiet moments with

God that had once kept me grounded. Sutton's search for peace was a mirror of my own in some ways, and it was humbling to realize that even though I was trying to guide him, I still had so much to learn. Maybe, just maybe, the very struggles we were facing, Sutton with his search for meaning, and me with my silent battles, weren't obstacles at all, but invitations. Invitations from a God who was quietly weaving His love into the cracks of our hearts, creating something far more beautiful than we could ever imagine. In that stillness, I realized that grace isn't something you earn, it's something you surrender to.

And maybe, that's what Sutton and I were both learning: that in our brokenness, we weren't meant to fix ourselves, but to let ourselves be found. It was the beginning of something far greater, something I was only just beginning to understand. Sitting there in the quiet, I knew one thing for certain: the God who brought us through our darkest days wasn't finished with us yet. And maybe, that was the greatest gift of all, knowing that even in the uncertainty, we were held by a love that wouldn't let go.

With every beat of my heart, I could feel the whisper of a truth I had nearly forgotten: that the same God who placed the stars in the sky was writing our story. And somehow, I knew He wasn't finished, not with me, not with Sutton, not with any of us. The night stretched on in perfect silence, but within me, something stirred, a quiet hope, a fragile faith, and the smallest flicker of a belief that this was only the beginning of a story we hadn't dared to dream yet.

And in that moment, as I sat in the dim light of my dorm room, I realized something extraordinary: sometimes, it's in the unraveling that God begins to weave His most beautiful work. After all, he had provided me with the family I have now, and I could not be more grateful.

The morning sunlight streamed through my window, warm and golden, spilling over my bed like a comforting blanket. I stretched my arms and sighed, feeling rested for the first time in what seemed like weeks. It was one of those mornings where everything felt just right, no rushing, no stress, just the calm rhythm of the world waking up.

After a quick prayer, I pulled on my favorite oversized sweater, the one that always made me feel a little more confident, and headed out the door with a smile. Today was going to be a good day. The air was crisp and cool, the kind that woke up your senses and made you feel alive.

As I walked across campus, I couldn't help but notice how beautiful everything looked. The leaves rustled softly in the breeze, and the faint aroma of coffee drifted from the café nearby. My heart felt light, like I was finally in sync with the world around me. I passed a few classmates and nodded at them, my smile widening when they smiled back.

Then I saw them. A group of girls I vaguely recognized from some of my classes walked toward me, their conversation interrupted by stifled laughter. I felt their eyes on me as they passed, and though their laughter wasn't loud, it felt sharp, pointed. I tried to brush it off, forcing my feet to keep moving, but the sting lingered. Were they laughing at me? My clothes? My hair? My heart sank a little, and the glow of the morning started to dim.

I pulled out my phone as soon as I was out of their sight, an old habit that I couldn't seem to shake when I felt uneasy. I found their Instagrams almost instinctively, scrolling through their perfectly curated feeds.

Picture after picture of them at the gym, on vacation, at parties.

Their smiles seemed effortless, their skin flawless, their bodies toned and lean in a way I'd never achieved no matter how hard I tried.

I couldn't stop comparing myself to them.

Their high cheekbones, their glowing skin, their sculpted arms and legs. Even their smiles seemed brighter and more genuine than mine.

It was like they belonged to a different world, one I could never step into no matter how much I tried. The more I scrolled, the worse I felt.

My stomach twisted as I looked down at myself. My sweater, which had felt cozy and cute just an hour ago, now felt frumpy and shapeless. My reflection in a nearby window felt like a cruel reminder of every flaw I couldn't unsee.

My hips felt too wide, my hair too plain, my face unremarkable.

"*You're not good enough*," the voice in my head whispered.

"*You'll never look like that.*"

"*You'll never be enough.*"

 I wanted to shake the thoughts away, but they stuck, replaying *over* and *over*.

By the time I slipped my phone back into my bag, the joy I'd felt earlier was gone. My heart felt heavy, my mood souring like milk left out in the sun. I didn't even want to look at anyone anymore, afraid that they were seeing the same flaws I couldn't stop obsessing over.

The rest of the walk felt like a blur. My good morning had unraveled so quickly, and all I could feel was disgust, at myself, at the way I let this happen, at the impossible standards I couldn't meet.

The voice in my head wouldn't stop.

 I wanted to cry, but even that felt like weakness. I kept walking, in what felt like circles. My mind raced with self-doubt, each thought like a stone thrown into a still pond, creating ripples that wouldn't stop spreading.

"*Why can't you look like them?*" I asked myself. "*Why can't you just be enough?*"

My chest tightened, and it felt like I was suffocating under the weight of everything I thought was wrong with me.

"*You'll never be as pretty as they are*," the voice hissed, "*You're just ordinary. Not special. Not worth noticing.*"

I clenched my fists at my sides, trying to shake off the words, but they stuck, like a layer of grime that wouldn't wash away.

"*I'll never fit in. I'll never be good enough,*"

I thought, the shame flooding in like a tidal wave, drowning out the good feelings I'd woken up with. I could feel the warmth leaving my body, replaced by a cold emptiness, a growing realization that I didn't like the person I saw when I looked in the mirror.

"Why can't I be more confident? Why can't I be stronger, like them?" I wondered. "*Why do I always feel so... invisible?*" It felt like there was a version of me that existed only in other people's eyes, a version I could never reach.

They were all so perfect, so put together, so effortless. And here I was, struggling just to hold myself together.

I hated how fragile I felt, how easily I crumbled under the weight of *comparison*.

How could anyone love someone like me? How could I ever love myself if all I saw was someone who didn't measure up?

I paused for a moment, the thoughts swirling in my head, and for a brief, fleeting second, I thought,

"*Maybe I don't even deserve to feel happy. Maybe I'm just meant to fade into the background.*"

The tears welled up in my eyes, but I blinked them away, unwilling to let anyone see how much I was breaking inside.

Instead, I tucked it all away, burying it deep, because who would care? Who would even notice?

I finally arrived to my class after walking what felt like the longest walk known to man-kind. I sat down at my desk, hoping no one would notice how I felt. I could still feel the sting of the girls' laughter echoing in my mind, like a low hum that wouldn't fade.

But then, I heard a voice, a familiar one, soft and concerned. "Claire, hey… are you okay?"

I turned to find Stella standing there, her eyes scanning me with a mix of worry and tenderness.

My stomach twisted. The last thing I wanted was for anyone to know something was wrong. The thought of people seeing through my mask and asking questions made my insides churn. I looked at her, trying to pull myself together, but I could feel the evidence of my tears still lingering beneath the surface, my eyes a little redder than usual.

"I-" I started, but my voice caught.

She had already seen it, hadn't she? I could feel her gaze piercing me, seeing more than I wanted her to.

"Did you cry? What's going on?" Stella asked, her voice soft, like she was afraid of pushing too hard.

I wanted to tell her everything, to let her see the pain I had tried to hide all morning.

But at the same time, I was terrified. What if she thought I was just seeking attention? What if everyone started noticing, asking questions, and I had to explain? What if they thought I just wanted pity? My chest tightened at the thought. I didn't want pity. I didn't want people to think I was weak or fragile or broken. I wasn't looking for anyone to feel sorry for me.

But deep down, I knew I couldn't pretend everything was fine.

Stella sat down beside me, her voice a little more insistent now. "You know I'm here for you, right? Whatever it is, you don't have to go through it alone."

I bit my lip, trying to keep my emotions in check, but it felt like I was holding back a flood. I wanted to say something, anything, but all I could think about was how much I didn't want to be a burden. How much I didn't want her to see me as the girl who always needed fixing. How much I just wanted to disappear, to not be the girl who had to be "taken care of."

Stella's words continued to echo in my mind, but they felt far away, distant, like I wasn't really present in the conversation. She was offering help, but part of me didn't feel like I deserved it.

"You've been glowing lately," she added. "And now… I don't know, you just seem different."

I felt a lump form in my throat. "Different" wasn't the word I would've used, but it was true. I felt like a version of myself that wasn't even worth noticing.

But what if I let her see how much I was struggling? What if that changed everything? Would she still look at me the same way? I closed my eyes for a moment, just wanting to disappear. The last thing I wanted was to be pitied. But could I really keep pretending? Could I keep pretending I wasn't falling apart on the inside?

Claire, your SO dramatic. I kept reminding myself.

 My head was still weighed down with everything that had happened, I tried to focus on the lecture in front of me. But I couldn't. My mind kept drifting, my exhaustion pulling me under like a current. I didn't even realize I had rested my head on my arms until I heard the sharp sound of my nurse aid teacher's voice.

"Claire," she said again. "You're not going to get anything out of this lecture with your head down like that. You need to stay focused."

 I straightened up quickly, my cheeks flushing. I didn't want to get in trouble, especially not now. But as I sat up, I couldn't hide how tired I was, how weighed down I felt. She paused for a moment, her sharp gaze softening as she looked at me more closely. I could feel her eyes scan my face, taking in the redness around my eyes, the way I was slouched in my seat.

The scolding tone she'd used before faded, and she asked, her voice gentler now, "Claire... are you okay? You look really tired. Do you need anything?"

For a brief second, I thought about just brushing it off, pretending I was fine.

But I couldn't. Something in her voice, the way she noticed me, really noticed me, made it feel okay to be vulnerable for a moment. I hesitated, unsure how to respond. Should I tell her? Should I explain why I felt so down? Or would that just make it worse? I swallowed hard, feeling the weight of their stares.

I wanted to be strong. I wanted to tell her I was fine, that everything was okay, and go back to pretending like I had it all together. But the more I thought about it, the more I felt like I was in a fishbowl, with everyone peering in, waiting for me to break.

I hesitated, my mind racing with the options. Should I tell her the truth? Would that make everything worse? Would I just become the girl who cried too much, who always needed someone to fix her?

Or should I lie, say I was fine, and retreat further into myself? I could feel the eyes of the whole room on me. The silence seemed to stretch, and I could almost hear their thoughts, the unspoken judgment hanging in the air. Was I that obvious? Did they all see how off I was today? I wanted to shrink, to hide from their gaze, but I couldn't. I smiled, and looked up at our teacher,

"Yes! I'm fine. Just tired, but thank you!"

I said hoping that would make everyone turn around, and just act as if I wasnt there.

"Oh- ok. You know how to reach me if you need anything." She answered, turning around and walking back towards the front of the class.

Ugh.

I felt miserable, and like I had the weight of *Jealousy* on my back.

The rest of the class felt like a blur, and the weight on my shoulders didn't lift, no matter how hard I tried to shake it off. The eyes of my classmates, the concern from my teacher, they all felt like too much, and I could feel myself sinking deeper into the spiral. But as I walked out of the classroom, I spotted him immediately, and heard myself sigh a sigh of relief. Sutton.

But as always, I felt the wrath of jealousy still on my back. *What if he thinks the same way those girls do? Or what if he sees me the same way I see myself?*

I remember thinking. He was strolling across the quad, his usual easy-going energy surrounding him. Just seeing him felt like a breath of fresh air, like I could finally exhale, like the heaviness in my chest might finally let go. Sutton and I had always been close, but today, I needed more than just a friend. I needed someone who wouldn't judge me for what I was feeling. As I walked toward him, my mind raced with the thoughts of everything I had been holding inside. The bitterness, the self-doubt, the shame. It all bubbled up in me again, but there was something about Sutton's presence that made the weight a little lighter, the air a little easier to breathe.

 Before I had walked out of the class a couple minutes before, I spotted the mirror that sat on the door. I looked exhausted, and sick. I remember the look on my face as I noticed that, and it was not easy to continue with the rest of my day. That would be my first thought before I went to approach Sutton. Great.

When he noticed me walking towards him, he flashed a smile, but his eyes quickly softened when he noticed the exhaustion in mine.

"Hey, Claire," he said, his voice warm, almost concerned. "Are you okay? You seem... off today. Are you sick?"

 I wanted to tell him everything, but I hesitated for a moment. What would he think of me? Would he pity me like everyone else? But his gentle gaze reassured me, and I found myself spilling it all, the worries, the hurt, the comparison. I told him about how I'd been feeling, how I couldn't stop comparing myself to everyone else, how I felt like I didn't belong, like I was just falling short in every way.

Before I could say a word, He said, "Come on, sit down. Let's talk."

We found a bench under a tree, and I sat down beside him, feeling the weight of everything still hanging on my shoulders. But Sutton didn't let it linger. He turned to me, his expression sincere and kind, and he looked right into my eyes.

"Claire, I'm not just saying this because I'm your friend," he said, his voice steady, "But you are beautiful. You are, truly. You don't see it, but I do."

He paused, letting the words sink in before continuing.

"And you're so much more than just what you see on the outside. You're a woman of Christ. You carry love and light in everything you do, and that makes you more radiant than anything else. Trust me when I say you're exactly who you're meant to be."

I blinked, surprised by how much weight his words carried.

"You don't have to say that," I started, but Sutton stopped me with a gentle shake of his head. "No, I'm serious, Claire," he said firmly. "It's not just about how you look or what you see when you look in the mirror. You're beautiful because of who you are on the inside. And the way you care for people, the way you have faith and love in everything you do, that's what makes you truly shine. Don't let anyone, or even yourself, make you think otherwise."

His words hit me deeper than I expected.

A part of me wanted to argue, to remind him how flawed I felt, but another part of me, the part that was starting to believe in what he was saying, felt lighter.

Slowly, the walls I had built around myself started to crack, and I felt the tension in my chest begin to ease. Sutton's words weren't just comforting; they were grounding. They reminded me that my worth wasn't tied to how I looked or how I measured up to anyone else. It was tied to who I was in Christ, to the love I gave, to the light I carried.

And in that moment, I started to believe it just a little bit more. The day didn't feel as heavy anymore. The comparisons didn't sting as much. And for the first time in what felt like forever,

I allowed myself to believe I was enough. I remembered my purpose, and why God had put me where I a today.

"You're here for a reason, Claire."

As that thought went through my mind, I felt a smile glide across my face, as I looked up at Sutton, and all that came out was, "Thank you." I have no clue if he knows how much that conversation helped me.

And I thank God for that interaction every day.

9

On a beautiful Sunday morning, I was heading to church, Kerri beside me in the passenger seat, just a couple of miles down the road from my dorm.

I stopped at the local Mcdonald's to grab a iced coffee to enjoy before I walked into church. About 20 minutes after I had settled into Church, to my surprise, Sutton showed up at church the following Sunday. He walked in wearing a button-down shirt and khakis, and honestly, I was thrilled to see him. He took a seat next to me in the pew, glancing around nervously as the service began. I offered him a warm smile, which he returned with a slight nod. It was subtle, but it was something. I couldn't help but feel a flutter in my chest as the worship music began.

As the chorus members sang, I found myself focusing less on the words and more on Sutton.

I prayed quietly in my heart, asking God to speak to him in ways I couldn't. *Lord, open Sutton's heart to Your truth. Let him feel Your presence today.*
I could feel Sutton's eyes on me. It was subtle, but I could sense his gaze lingering every now and then, as if he was trying to figure out how I could be so at

peace. As the pastor began the sermon about grace and redemption, something shifted in me. I felt like God was giving me a message to share with Sutton.

At the end of the sermon, after the closing prayer, I turned toward him slowly, my heart pounding with the words I felt were meant for him. Sutton was still staring straight ahead, his expression thoughtful, but distant.

"Sutton," I said softly, touching his arm.

He turned toward me, and for a moment, we were silent. I could see the skepticism still clouding his eyes, but there was also a flicker of something else, something deeper, something yearning.

"I know this is all a lot to take in," I began, "but I want you to understand something. *Through Him, we are redeemed, Sutton.* He forgives us, no matter what we've done. That's the power of grace."

The words seemed to hang in the air, and I could see his whole body tense up. Sutton's eyes widened slightly, and it was as if a weight had just landed on him.

For a moment, I could feel the world pause around us. His breath caught in his throat, and his hand trembled slightly as he wiped his face, but I could see that it wasn't from the cool air in the church. It was from something deeper.

Something stirring inside him. I watched, mesmerized, as tears began to fall down his face, one by one, catching the light like diamonds as they traced his jawline.

My own heart *ached* seeing him so vulnerable, so broken, but so beautiful in this moment.

Sutton, the confident quarterback, the guy who never let anyone see his emotions, was broken open before me. His eyes locked with mine, and for the first time, I saw something shift in him, a softness, a willingness to receive.

"I don't know what to do with this," he whispered, his voice cracking.

"You don't have to do anything right now. Just know that He loves you, Sutton. That's enough. His love is enough."

Sutton's eyes fluttered shut for a brief moment, and I could tell his mind was racing. He was processing it all, he was letting it in. I reached out and placed my hand on his, offering him a quiet support that words couldn't quite capture.

The quiet weight of the moment felt sacred.

And then, as the silence between us deepened, I heard him whisper, a quiet breath escaping his lips, "Thank you, Claire."

In that instant, my heart soared, and I realized that God had used me to plant a seed of truth in Sutton's heart. Maybe that was the beginning of something more, something lasting. But for now, I was content knowing that Sutton had heard the gospel and that his heart had been moved. It wasn't the end of his journey, but it was a step, a beautiful, powerful step toward redemption. And for the first time in a long while, I felt certain that Sutton would find his way back to God's love.

As I sat there, my hand still resting gently on his, I could feel the weight of everything he had been carrying. Sutton was always so composed, so confident in front of others, but in that moment, I could see the cracks in his armor.

 He had a hunger for something more, something beyond the surface. It wasn't just the doubts or the questions that had lingered in his mind for years; it was the deep longing in his heart for peace, for acceptance, for something to anchor him in the midst of his chaos.

I could tell he was wrestling with all the things he thought he had to fix about himself before he could even approach God. But that was the thing, wasn't it? It wasn't about being perfect; it was about being willing. The words from the sermon kept echoing in my mind, grace and redemption.

I realized that Sutton needed to hear those words in
the rawest form. He didn't need a lecture or another
reason to feel like he wasn't enough.

He needed to hear that God saw him as he was,
broken, yes, but loved all the same. I could see how
the idea of grace was difficult for him to grasp. He had
always been someone who depended on his strength,
his achievements, his control. It was hard for him to let
go and trust that God's love didn't depend on how
much he could do or how well he could hide his flaws.

I watched as his eyes flickered between the floor and
me, his mind clearly sorting through the truth I had just
shared with him. It was as if everything he had tried to
fill the empty spaces in his heart with had failed him,
and now he was faced with a love he couldn't quite
comprehend but knew he needed.

The raw vulnerability in his expression broke me open,
and I realized in that moment that Sutton was longing
for the very thing I had in my heart, faith, peace, and a
sense of belonging.

I could see the walls coming down piece by piece, like
he was slowly allowing himself to believe that he
could come as he was, without needing to be anything
more. God was softening his heart, and it was one of
the most beautiful things I had ever witnessed. It was
then that I knew that this moment, as simple as it
seemed, could change the course of his life. Sutton was
beginning to let go of the weight he had carried for so

long, and in doing so, he was starting to open himself to God's love.

The journey wasn't over, and I couldn't expect him to have all the answers right then and there, but I knew this was a pivotal moment.

Sutton was no longer just the quarterback with everything together; he was a young man realizing that the greatest strength he could have was admitting his need for God.

And I had the privilege of walking beside him as he took this first step. I had always known Sutton carried a weight, though it wasn't until that Sunday morning in church that I began to truly understand the extent of it. As a football player, Sutton was expected to be a leader, strong, confident, and always composed. The pressure on him to perform, not just for his team but for everyone around him, was immense. He was the star quarterback of the University of North Carolina's football team, and with that came an enormous responsibility. His every move on the field was watched by coaches, fans, and teammates, each hoping to see him succeed. The long hours of practice, the relentless training sessions, the constant pressure to be the best, it all seemed to consume him.

But despite his success, I could see the strain it was causing him. His life wasn't just about football; it was about living up to the expectations that came with it. Alongside that, he had academic goals, he wanted to be a doctor, and I could see how much he struggled to juggle both. Football practices, game preparations, and late-night study sessions left him little time to rest or reflect. He was always rushing from one commitment to the next, barely catching his breath. And I could see how overwhelmed he felt. For someone who was used to being in control, to be this consumed by pressure, it seemed to be breaking him down, little by little. Even with all of this, I never gave up on Sutton. I could see how hard he was trying, how much he was pushing himself, but I also saw the cracks in his armor.

Sutton was someone who liked to keep his emotions in check, always maintaining a strong exterior. But I could tell that it was getting harder for him to keep everything together. He was wrestling with more than just the stress of school and football; he was grappling with something deeper. I could feel it in the way he sometimes looked at me, as if he was searching for something, something he couldn't quite name. It made me realize just how much I needed to continue praying for him.

And as my own life became increasingly hectic, I found that my faith was being tested, too. Between the pressure of schoolwork, my clinical hours, and my future as a NICU nurse, I could feel myself being pulled in every direction. I had always prided myself on balancing my faith with my academic and personal life, but the reality of senior year was proving to be more challenging than I anticipated. I would often find myself feeling overwhelmed, wondering how I was going to make it through. It wasn't easy to keep my focus on God when the world around me felt so chaotic.

Yet, every time I felt that anxiety creeping in, I would turn to prayer, knowing that it was the one thing I could rely on. I prayed for strength, for clarity, and for peace amidst the chaos. It wasn't always easy, but I knew that God would give me the resilience I needed to keep going. Sutton, however, was still far from understanding the peace I had found.

As I watched him that Sunday in church, his face clouded with skepticism yet marked by a quiet longing, I knew that he was struggling with something more than just the overwhelming weight of his schedule. The idea of faith, of surrendering to God's grace, was a foreign concept to him. He had always been someone who relied on his own strength, someone who believed that he had to earn everything, even love and forgiveness. The thought of letting go and trusting in a love he couldn't control was difficult for him to grasp. In that moment, I could see the conflict within him, the tension between his desire for control and the deep longing he had for something more, something that couldn't be achieved through his own efforts. It was as if he wanted to believe but wasn't sure if he could let himself.

He was used to being the one who fixed everything, the one who had all the answers. But as I shared those words of grace with him, I could see his walls beginning to crumble. It was the first time I saw Sutton truly vulnerable, and it broke my heart. In his tears, I saw the conviction beginning to stir inside him, the realization that he didn't have to be perfect to receive God's love. That love wasn't something he had to earn; it was a gift, freely given. I could see that Sutton was beginning to understand that, and it gave me hope. In the weeks that followed, I noticed small changes in Sutton. He was still trying to figure things out, still wrestling with his faith, but there was something different about him.

He was quieter, more reflective.

When we studied together, he would ask questions about God, about grace, and what it really meant to follow Jesus. At first, I wasn't sure if he was just curious or if he was starting to let his guard down, but I knew it was a step in the right direction. Sutton had always been someone who depended on his strength, his success on the football field, his academic achievements, his ability to control his environment.

But now, he was starting to realize that he didn't have all the answers, and that was okay. It was hard for him to accept that he couldn't fix everything himself, especially when it came to matters of faith. But I could see that he was slowly coming to terms with it. There were moments when I could feel the weight of his questions, the intensity with which he was searching for meaning. He was looking for something that could ground him, something that could give him peace in the midst of all the chaos. And as I continued to walk beside him, I prayed that God would meet him in his searching, that He would provide the answers that Sutton was seeking.

For me, the journey of maintaining my own faith while supporting Sutton was both challenging and rewarding. There were moments when I felt like I couldn't keep up with everything, when my schoolwork felt like it was piling up and my prayers for Sutton seemed unanswered. But I kept trusting that God had a plan for both of us. I couldn't control Sutton's journey to faith, but I could be there for him, offering love, encouragement, and prayer. It wasn't easy, but I knew that God was using me in ways I couldn't always see.

As I walked alongside Sutton, I knew that my role wasn't to force him into faith but to show him the love and grace that had changed my life. It was a slow process, but every conversation, every prayer, every moment of support, was a step closer to seeing Sutton embrace the peace that I had found in Christ. And through it all, I reminded myself that my faith, too, needed to be nurtured. I had to trust that God was with me, that He would provide the strength I needed to continue. I prayed not only for Sutton but for myself, that my own faith would remain steadfast in the face of all the challenges life threw my way.

As I was drifting asleep, I caught myself looking at my high school journal. The journal that held my prayers, my drive, and my.. Crushes? I knew right then I had to get up and look at it, and just look through it I told myself, just looking.

As I began to read, one page read, "I caught myself smiling whenever I saw him, the way his laugh seemed to fill the room and how he always knew just what to say to make me feel seen, even if he didn't know how much I was falling for him in those moments."

Yuck. I knew exactly who that was about.

After I got over my journal, I knew what had to be done, I had to write SOMETHING.

I let my pen write whatever my mind desired, and the first words came out to say, "I caught myself smiling whenever I saw him, the way his laugh seemed to fill the room and how he always knew just what to say to make me feel seen, even if he didn't know how much I was falling for him in those moments."

Claire Thompson.

I remember thinking to myself. I closed my journal quick, and aggressively. The weight of the moment settled over me like a blanket, not heavy, but comforting.

Outside my window, the campus lay cloaked in quiet, the moonlight glinting off frost-kissed rooftops. It felt as though the world had paused, holding its breath for whatever was to come next. And in that stillness, I realized something that made my heart ache with its simplicity: Sutton wasn't just searching for something greater, he was part of something greater. So was I. God was at work, weaving together our stories with threads of grace, purpose, and love in ways I couldn't yet see. I thought of all the moments that had brought me here, the laughter, the tears, the prayers whispered in the dead of night. I thought of Sutton's vulnerability, the quiet crack in his armor that hinted at a deeper longing.

And I thought of how God had a way of meeting us in those cracks, turning our brokenness into something beautiful. The beauty of faith isn't in the answers we find, it's in the questions we dare to ask, the steps we take when the way ahead is unclear, and the quiet hope that whispers: Keep going. I am with you.

As I lay back on my pillow, a sense of peace washed over me, deeper than anything I had felt in months. Sutton's journey wasn't mine to control, but I could be part of it, by being present, by praying, by loving him in a way that reflected the love of Christ. Because at the heart of it all, that's what faith is: not a destination, but a journey. And maybe, just maybe, the most extraordinary moments happen when we let go of our need to know where the road leads and trust the One who walks beside us. The night stretched long and silent, but my heart was anything but still. I whispered one final prayer before sleep claimed me: "Lord, let Your light shine in the darkest places. And if it be Your will, let me be a part of it." I didn't know what tomorrow would bring. But in that moment, I wasn't afraid. I wasn't uncertain. I wasn't alone. I was His. And that was enough. It was Sutton Adams. That was my purpose.

10

Sutton and I's late-night talks became a sanctuary for me.

It was during those quiet, still moments, long after the world had fallen asleep, that I felt a deep connection with Sutton. He was genuinely searching, asking questions that required me to dig deeper into my own faith, and I welcomed that. It felt like a part of my prayer for him, my prayer for truth to reveal itself in his heart, was beginning to unfold. Every conversation felt like a small victory, a step forward in him seeing the world through a new lens.

And as those conversations continued, I couldn't help but feel grateful. I had prayed for years for my friends to understand the depth of God's love, and here, right before me, was a moment I had longed for. I could sense it in the air, Sutton was on the edge of something, a change that was beyond words, a change only God could orchestrate. I could see how much those talks meant to him as well. His expressions sometimes revealed a longing to believe but also a fear of surrender. Yet, I knew in my heart that everything we had talked about, every ounce of truth that had spilled out of my lips, was what he needed.

Every time he asked a hard question, I prayed for clarity in my answers. It wasn't about me convincing him; it was about God revealing Himself to him in a way Sutton could understand.

In the moments when I felt overwhelmed, I would pray quietly to myself: "Lord, show him Your truth. Open his heart to the beauty of Your grace. Give him peace where there is doubt."

I prayed not just for Sutton but for Kelli, for everyone who was searching, or even those who didn't know they were searching yet. I prayed for my own growth, too, because I realized that these moments weren't just about Sutton's faith journey. They were about mine as well. One evening, as I sat in my room, reflecting on all that had happened in the past few weeks, I felt a deep sense of peace. What I had been praying for, what I had hoped for so much, was happening. Sutton was coming to a place where he could see God more clearly.

There was no doubt in my mind that God had been preparing his heart all along, even before I knew him. My prayers weren't just words; they were being answered, in ways both big and small.

 The transformation in Sutton wasn't instant, and I knew it wasn't going to be. But there was something special about seeing the sparks of faith begin to light up in him. It wasn't about trying to fix him, it was about walking alongside him, offering what I had learned through my own walk with Christ.

And I could see it in his eyes, the subtle shift, the quiet change that said, "Maybe this is real. Maybe there is something to this after all."

As much as I loved these talks, I knew it wasn't all about deep discussions and moments of reflection. Life continued moving forward, and sometimes it was the simplest of experiences that could bring about powerful realizations.

That Saturday morning, Kelli and I were getting ready to head to a historical church downtown. I had been looking forward to this trip for weeks.

The church was supposed to be stunning, one of the oldest in the area, and I was eager to experience its history and the rich sense of peace it exuded. We had planned to make a day of it, touring the church, learning its history, and soaking in its beauty. As we left the dorm, we ran into a group of guys from a nearby sorority who immediately took an interest in us.

At first, it was harmless small talk, but the conversation quickly took a turn that made both Kelli and me uneasy.

The guys started making suggestive comments about the sorority and asking if we wanted to join them for drinks afterward. "Come on, it'll be fun," one of them said with a smirk. "You don't have to go to church, right? You can come hang out with us instead."

I could feel my stomach tighten, but I kept calm. Kelli looked at me, unsure of how to respond, but I stood firm.

"We're not interested," I said. "We're heading to a church, and we'd appreciate it if you left us alone."

The guys chuckled, clearly mocking me.

"What are you, some kind of saint?" one of them sneered.

The others laughed, and I could feel Kelli shrink a little in the face of their teasing.

But I stayed firm. "We're not looking for trouble," I said, "And we're not ashamed of our faith."

They scoffed and turned away, muttering about our "Religion."

I stood tall, though, feeling a sense of pride in how I handled the situation. It wasn't about proving something to them; it was about staying true to who I was and what I believed.

Kelli, however, seemed a little shaken. She wasn't as comfortable with confrontation, and I could see she felt awkward about how I had shut them down.

"You were pretty blunt back there," she said, her voice soft. "I don't know if I would've been that harsh."

I nodded. "Maybe it wasn't the nicest way to put it, but we don't owe them an explanation. Our faith is a part of us, Kelli. We don't need to hide that for anyone."

Kelli looked at me, uncertain. "I just feel like I should've been more... polite. I don't want to offend anyone."

I smiled gently. "There's no reason to be ashamed of our faith, Kelli. We're not ashamed to stand firm in what we believe. If anything, we have the love of God to guide us, and that's something to be proud of."

As we finally made our way into the church, I felt a peaceful reassurance wash over me. The space inside was breathtaking, high vaulted ceilings, intricate stained glass windows that let in beams of colorful light, and pews worn smooth by years of prayer and devotion. It was a place steeped in history and grace, and I couldn't help but feel deeply moved. We took our time, walking quietly through the space, each of us taking in the serenity and beauty around us.

The church was a reminder of the lasting power of faith through centuries. I could see how the generations before us had found solace in this sacred place, and I felt privileged to be there. Kelli seemed to relax, her worries forgotten as she gazed around in awe at the stained glass and towering columns. It was a good experience, one that left both of us with a sense of gratitude and awe.

Later, as we walked out into the crisp afternoon air, I turned to Kelli. "You know, there's nothing to be embarrassed about in what we did earlier. We stood up for what we believe, and there's no shame in that." Kelli nodded slowly, still thoughtful.

"I guess I just don't always know how to handle situations like that. It feels like we're being judged for something we can't control."

"You're right," I said gently. "But remember, God's love is eternal. It doesn't depend on what people think of us. And His love is more than enough. When you stand firm in Him, you can face anything with confidence. We don't need to seek earthly approval, Kelli. We already have the approval of the One who matters most."

Kelli smiled faintly, and I could see the wheels turning in her mind. I knew it wasn't easy for her to always stand firm in her faith, but I also knew that over time, she would come to understand just how precious and unshakable God's love was.

"Thanks, Claire," she said quietly. "I needed to hear that."

When we got back to the dorms, I couldn't sit still. I has been standing in the shower for almost an hour, when my mind drifted to Sutton, again. When I got out of he shower, and dried off, I told Sutton to meet me at the coffee shop we always met at. That evening after one of our talks, I looked at Sutton, and for a split second, I felt a warmth flood through me. He was sitting across from me, rubbing his hand through his hair, his eyes focused on the ground as he thought about everything we'd just discussed. For a moment, he looked vulnerable, not the quarterback with everything under control, but just a guy who was trying to figure out life.

I couldn't help myself. "You know," I said, my voice teasing yet soft, "I think you're more of a softie than you let on. There's more to you than that tough guy exterior."

Sutton's eyes flickered to mine, and a smirk tugged at the corner of his mouth. "You're just saying that because I've been asking all these deep questions," he replied. "But, maybe you're right. I can't always be the tough guy. Sometimes, it's easier to talk about football than about what's really going on inside."

I felt my heart soften at his honesty. "You know, Sutton, if you ever need a break from football talk, I'm always here. And maybe I'll even let you win a game of chess one of these days."

He laughed, and for a moment, it felt like the world outside us disappeared. As Sutton leaned forward, his elbows resting on the small coffee shop table, I couldn't help but notice the way his questions always carried a hint of vulnerability. It wasn't just curiosity, it was a search, a longing to understand something greater than himself.

His eyes, usually so guarded, had softened, and I could see the conflict there: the push and pull between wanting to believe and fearing what surrender might mean.

"I guess what I don't understand," he said, his voice quieter now, "Is how you can be so sure. How do you know it's all real?"

I took a deep breath, praying silently for the right words. "It's not about having all the answers," I said. "It's about trust. Surrendering to God isn't about giving up, it's about letting go of the need to control everything and trusting that He's got a better plan, even when we can't see it."

Sutton studied me, his brow furrowing as he processed my words. "Letting go sounds terrifying," he admitted, his voice barely above a whisper.

"It is," I said, nodding. "But it's also freeing. When you surrender, you're not alone anymore. You're trusting Someone who loves you more than you could ever imagine, who wants what's best for you, even when you can't see it. It's like... stepping into the unknown but knowing you'll be caught."

His eyes held mine for a moment, and I could see something shift, a tiny crack in the walls he'd built around his heart.

As the hours went on,we walked side by side under the streetlights, I found myself reflecting on how safe I felt with Sutton. It wasn't just the way he had stepped between me and those boys earlier or the way he always seemed to be looking out for me. It was something deeper. Sutton had this quiet strength, a presence that made me feel like I could let my guard down. Being around him reminded me of surrendering to God, in a way. It wasn't about everything being perfect or easy, it was about trust. With Sutton, I didn't feel like I had to have everything figured out. I could just be me, flaws and all, and that was enough. It was a kind of safety I hadn't expected to find in him, but it was there, steady and unshakable, like the faith I was learning to lean on more every day. The experience at the church that Saturday morning was a turning point for me, too. I didn't realize just how much I needed that space until we walked inside. The church's grandeur, the history etched into its stone walls, and the calmness that washed over me as I took in the stained glass windows, it all reminded me of the power of standing firm in my faith. I felt connected to generations of believers who had walked the same paths, prayed the same prayers, and sought the same peace. It gave me a renewed sense of purpose, and I realized that I wasn't just walking this path for myself, I was walking it for everyone I cared about, especially Sutton. I wanted him to find that peace, to stand firm in his faith, just as I was learning to.

As dark came, it got harder and harder to see our surroundings. Randomly, Sutton unexpectedly grasped my hand, gently pulling me slightly behind him as he stepped in front of me. Just as we were walking out onto the sidewalk, a group of men jumped out from the corner, grinning ear to ear as they blocked our path, clearly thinking they were being funny.

Sutton didn't hesitate, standing tall between me and the boys, his protective instinct kicking in as he subtly shifted his body to shield me, his hand still firmly holding mine. The boys chuckled and made some snarky comments, but Sutton didn't flinch.

His grip on my hand tightened just a little, and his posture remained solid, exuding an unspoken confidence that left no room for their games.

I could feel the energy shift, their mocking smiles faltered for a moment, and the tension in the air was palpable. For a split second, I thought one of them might take a step forward, but Sutton's steady gaze kept them at bay. It was strange, in a way, seeing this side of Sutton.

He was usually so laid-back and focused on football, but right now, his presence was strong, protective. As the boys hesitated, their smirks slowly fading, I could sense Sutton's unspoken message: we weren't going to be messed with.

Eventually, they shrugged and moved out of the way, muttering under their breath, but I couldn't help but feel a sense of gratitude for Sutton's quiet bravery. His protective side had always been there, but it was in moments like this that it felt especially real.

As the boys walked off, Sutton kept his hand firmly in mine, his thumb gently rubbing over my knuckles as if to reassure me. I glanced up at him, a little surprised by how natural his protective instinct had felt.

He gave me a small, almost teasing smile, though his eyes still held a trace of concern. "You alright?" Sutton asked, his voice low, but steady.

"Yeah," I said, nodding quickly. "I'm fine. Thanks for stepping in, though. That was... sweet."

Sutton gave a small shrug, his expression softening. "What else was I supposed to do? Let them keep messing with you?"

He let out a light laugh, but there was a hint of something more serious beneath it. "I'm not about to let anyone make you feel uncomfortable. Not if I can help it haha."

I couldn't help but feel a flutter in my chest at his words. There was something in the way he said them, like he genuinely meant it.

"Well, I appreciate it," I said quietly, meeting his gaze.

"You've always had my back, haven't you?"

Sutton's smile widened, though he tried to hide the pride in his eyes.

"Yeah. Guess I have," he replied, his voice softening. "It's kind of my thing. Looking out for the people I care about."

I couldn't help but laugh lightly, the tension from the earlier moment starting to lift.

"Good thing I'm on that list, huh?"

"Definitely," Sutton said, his voice taking on a playful tone as he nudged me gently with his shoulder.

"You're lucky I'm so nice." He said.

"Uh-huh," I said with a grin, though a little warmth crept into my cheeks.

"I'll remember that the next time I need saving." I joked.

Sutton raised an eyebrow. "You'll know who to call."

He winked, the flirtation obvious now, and my heart skipped a beat. He was joking, but there was something in the way he said it, something genuine, like he'd really be there, no matter what. I smiled back at him, feeling a sense of calm that only seemed to come when I was with him.

"Thanks, Sutton," I said softly, letting the moment hang in the air.

"Anytime, Claire," he replied, his voice serious again, though there was a touch of warmth in his eyes that made it clear his offer wasn't just for show.

It was real. When we arrived back to the campus, Sutton let go of the grasping of my sweaty palm from the 2 block walk from the coffee shop, to the campus.

"Had a great time, let me know if you ever need anything, Claire."

Sutton had said these words so effortlessly, and without hesitation he hugged me, and looked down at me with those blue breath-takimng eyes.

"Thank you, Sutton. Me too."

As Sutton pulled away from the hug, he hesitated for a moment, his hand lingering on my arm.

"You know," he said, his voice softer now, "I don't think I've ever met anyone like you, Claire."

I felt my breath catch, his words catching me off guard.

"What do you mean?" I asked, my voice barely above a whisper.

He glanced down, almost as if gathering his thoughts. "You just... you make me want to be better," he admitted, his blue eyes meeting mine.

"It's like you see something in me that I didn't even know was there."

My heart swelled at his honesty, and I couldn't help but smile.

"That's because I do see it, Sutton. You're capable of so much more than you realize."

He gave a small, almost shy laugh, rubbing the back of his neck.

"You've got a lot of faith in me, huh?"

"I do," I said firmly, not breaking his gaze. "And one day, I think you'll see what I see, too."

For a moment, we just stood there, the world around us fading away. Then Sutton took a deep breath, his expression softening.

"Thanks for believing in me, Claire. It means more than you know."

"Always," I replied, my voice steady. "I'm here for you, Sutton. No matter what."

As he nodded, a faint smile playing on his lips, I knew that this moment wasn't just about words, it was about something deeper, something unspoken but real.

"Goodnight, Claire," he said finally, his voice low and warm.

"Goodnight, Sutton," I replied, watching as he turned and walked away, the evening air cool against my skin but my heart impossibly full.

And with that, I turned to walk inside, a sense of warmth spreading through me, knowing that tomorrow would bring yet another step forward, together.

11

A three-day weekend felt like a gift I didn't realize I needed until I was already packing my bag.

It had been weeks since I'd last gone home, and the thought of seeing my family filled me with warmth. The drive wasn't far, maybe forty minutes, but every mile closer felt like stepping back into a part of myself I hadn't visited in a while.

When I pulled into the driveway, the sound of laughter hit me before I even opened my car door. Collins and Crew, my little brothers, were racing around the yard, their voices carrying in the crisp afternoon air.

"Claire!" Collins yelled, running toward me with Crew right behind him.

Their arms wrapped around me in a tight hug, and I laughed, ruffling their hair. "Missed you guys," I said, pulling them close.

"Mom said we're making alfredo tonight!" Crew announced, his face lighting up with excitement.

"Of course she is," I said, grinning. "She knows it's my favorite."

Inside, the house smelled like home, a mix of cinnamon from the diffuser my mom loved and a faint hint of freshly baked cookies.

My mom greeted me with a warm hug, her eyes crinkling at the corners. "You look tired, sweetheart. College treating you okay?"

"It's fine, Mom. Just busy," I said, following her into the kitchen.

The smells I had once embraced every day, enveloped me, instantly easing the tension of my hectic college life. The house, a harmonious blend of modern design and familial warmth, stood as a testament to my parents' meticulous care. The open-concept living area featured sleek, contemporary furniture softened by plush throw pillows and cozy blankets, creating an inviting atmosphere.

Natural light streamed through large windows, casting a gentle glow on the polished hardwood floors, while subtle touches of greenery added a refreshing vibrancy to the space. Our kitchen, the heart of the home, was a perfect fusion of style and function. State-of-the-art appliances gleamed beneath under-cabinet lighting, and the expansive island, adorned with a vase of fresh flowers, beckoned for family gatherings. The aroma of my mother's cooking filled the air, a comforting reminder of countless meals shared around the table.

 I couldn't help but feel a pang of longing for the simplicity and comfort of living under my parents' roof. The thought of returning to my own apartment, with its sterile, minimalist decor and the constant hum of city life, seemed less appealing in the face of the warmth and familiarity that enveloped me here.

As I settled into the cozy nook by the window, a cup of my mother's homemade hot chocolate in hand, I reflected on the subtle art of creating a home that balances modern aesthetics with familial comfort. Incorporating natural elements like wood accents and soft textiles can add warmth to a modern space, making it feel inviting and lived-in. The strategic use of lighting, layering ambient, task, and accent lights, can transform a room, casting a soft glow that enhances its cozy ambiance. Personal touches, such as family photographs and heirloom pieces, infuse the space with character and a sense of belonging. These elements, thoughtfully combined, create a sanctuary that not only reflects personal style but also nurtures the soul. In this haven, I found solace and a sense of belonging that my apartment could never provide.

The warmth of my family's presence, the comforting embrace of a well-loved home, and the simple joys of shared moments reminded me of the importance of creating spaces that nourish the heart and spirit. We spent the afternoon catching up, chatting about everything and nothing while shopping at the local city square. It was one of my favorite things to do with her, walking through the small boutiques, picking out little trinkets, and laughing over things we didn't need but wanted anyway. She bought me a scarf, soft and warm, and insisted it would be perfect for the cooler mornings.

I heard what sounded like rustling around of coins, and as it caught my attention, my gaze was drawn to the delicate pocket watch resting in my mothers hands, that she had pulled from her pocket.

"A gift from my mother, a cherished heirloom that had been passed down through generations." She said, showing me its polished brass case gleamed softly in the ambient light, the intricate engravings on its surface telling stories of time's passage and the hands that had held it before me.

Suspended from a slender, gold-plated chain, the watch exuded an air of timeless elegance. The chain, with its subtle sheen, was both functional and ornamental, designed to keep the watch secure while adding a touch of sophistication. Its length was perfect for draping over a waistcoat or slipping into a pocket, making it a versatile accessory that blended seamlessly with both formal attire and casual wear.

Opening the watch revealed a classic white dial adorned with Roman numerals, their black ink contrasting sharply against the pristine background. The delicate hands, finely crafted and slender, moved gracefully over the face, marking the passage of time with a gentle sweep. At the center, a small subdial indicated the seconds, its rhythmic ticking a constant reminder of life's fleeting moments. The back of the watch was equally captivating, featuring a transparent case back that offered a glimpse into the intricate mechanical movement within. The gears and springs, meticulously arranged, worked in harmony to keep time, a testament to the craftsmanship and precision that had gone into its creation. This transparent design not only showcased the watchmaker's art but also symbolized the transparency and trust that had been passed down through my family.

As I held the watch, I was reminded of my mother's words: "Keep it, in remembrance of *God's timing*."

This heirloom was more than just a timepiece; it was a tangible connection to my family's history and a constant reminder of the divine timing that governs our lives. Each tick of the watch was a gentle nudge to trust in the journey, to have faith in the path laid out before me, and to remember that, in the grand tapestry of life, every moment is woven with purpose and grace.

The gold pocket watch, with its blend of functionality and beauty, served as a daily reminder of the importance of patience and trust in God's plan. Its presence in my life was a source of comfort and inspiration, a symbol of the enduring love and wisdom of my mother, and a cherished heirloom that would continue to be passed down, carrying with it the stories and lessons of those who had come before.

That evening, after dinner, my dad and I sat outside on the porch swing. The sky was painted in hues of orange and pink as the sun dipped below the horizon. "It's beautiful," I said, resting my head against his shoulder.

"God's artistry," he replied with a smile. "You know, Claire, there was a time in my life when I didn't notice sunsets like this. I was too busy chasing things that didn't matter. But one day, God got my attention in a way I couldn't ignore. I was driving home late from work, frustrated about something that didn't go my way, and it started to rain. For some reason, I pulled over on the side of the road, and I just broke down. I cried out to Him, told Him I couldn't do it on my own anymore. And right then, the rain stopped, and the clouds parted just enough for the sun to break through. It was like God was saying, 'I've got you.' From that day on, I've trusted Him in a way I never had before."

 I looked up at him, feeling a lump form in my throat. "Thank you for sharing that, Dad."

He patted my hand. "It's moments like these that remind me of His faithfulness, Claire. Never forget that He's always with you."

 I decided on staying home that night, in my old room. I remember thinking,

"*This is really like a time frozen room. How has the time went by so fast? So unfair, time is a thief.*"

The air felt unnervingly cold, almost as if the space had been trapped in time. I couldn't explain it, it was late at night, and the warmth of the sun should have been spilling through the windows. But here, in this room, there was only an oppressive stillness, a heaviness in the air that made me pause. It was as if the walls themselves were holding their breath, waiting for something, someone, to stir it back to life. The walls were painted in muted beige, with soft green accents, the colors neutral but timeless. The furniture was old, worn, but still intact, as if it had been carefully preserved for a life that had never really continued. There was a table near the door, covered in delicate china cups, the edges of each one faintly chipped. The soft light coming through the blinds barely touched the room, leaving it shrouded in a quiet gloom that matched the silence. I walked into the space slowly, my feet hesitant as I took it all in. There was something eerie about this room, something that made me feel like I had stepped into a different world, one that didn't belong to the present. I ran my hand over the back of an armchair, the fabric dusty and slightly stiff. It had once been soft and inviting, but now it felt neglected, like everything else in here. The house had once been full of life, I could tell. I almost felt as if I could hear echoes of conversations, voices that had once filled the air with warmth and laughter. But now, there was nothing but silence. I moved toward a bookshelf in the corner, the wood worn smooth from age but still strong.

Books were lined up neatly, as if someone had made sure everything was in place, even though they hadn't been touched in a long time. My fingers traced the spines, and I noticed a well-worn Bible. The cover had faded with time, but it still had a certain beauty. I pulled it off the shelf carefully, opening it to a random page, the pages stiff from years of being closed. I ran my thumb over the words, feeling the weight of them in my hands, the promises they carried.

The clock on the mantelpiece caught my eye. Its hands were stuck, frozen at a time long passed. The silence felt even heavier with that broken clock, reminding me that time here had stopped. The ticking was gone. But there was something almost sacred about it, this room frozen in place. I felt a strange reverence, as if the stillness was a quiet prayer in itself, one I could almost hear if I listened hard enough.

I walked further into the room, my gaze falling on a photograph hanging on the wall. It was a family portrait, two parents, a child, all smiling with the carefree joy that comes from being together. The edges of the frame were chipped, and the faces in the photo had begun to fade. I wondered about their story. Where were they now? What had happened to this room, once filled with love and connection? I closed my eyes for a moment, offering a silent prayer. I prayed for them, whoever they were, that God would heal whatever was broken, that He would restore what had been lost. I prayed for this room, too, that it wouldn't remain cold and still forever.

As I moved deeper into the room, I noticed something familiar, something that brought a wave of warmth and nostalgia rushing through me. On the small side table near the window, beneath a layer of dust, lay my old Bible, the leather cover cracked from years of use. I hadn't seen it in so long. It was the one I used during my high school years, its pages filled with underlined verses and notes, remnants of all the mornings I had spent sitting with God, studying His word and asking for guidance. It was strange, seeing it here, in this room frozen in time, as if it had been waiting for me to return. Beside it, scattered around carelessly, were my old Bible study papers. The papers I had scribbled on in my youth, full of half-formed thoughts and reflections, prayers I had written during moments of doubt and joy. They were still there, just as I had left them years ago, crumpled edges, ink faded but still readable.

A sense of peace washed over me as I picked up one of the papers, reading a prayer I had written when I was struggling through a tough season. It felt so distant now, but I remembered the rawness of those feelings. How simple yet powerful those moments had been, leaning on my faith, trusting in God even when I didn't fully understand everything. The papers had once been spread out across this very table as I spent hours diving into God's word, learning more about who He was and what He wanted from me. It felt like no time had passed at all as I looked at them, just like they had been left yesterday. There was something so sacred in that moment, standing here in this room, where everything had been left just as it was, waiting. My heart swelled as I ran my fingers over the worn pages, feeling the connection to my past self, to the girl I had been. I knew she was still there inside me, that her prayers still mattered, her faith still counted. It was a reminder that even in the stillness, even when life seems to freeze, God's presence remains constant.

Through all the papers, my old Bible, though aged and worn, reminded me that my journey of faith wasn't finished. It had only grown, and the foundation I had built through these very things was still with me. They were a sign of how much I had changed and how far I had come, but also a promise that God had been with me all along, guiding me through each chapter of my life.

As I gently placed the Bible back on the table and smoothed out one of the papers, I said a prayer right there in the room, surrounded by the remnants of my past. I prayed that God would continue to guide me, just as He had when I was a teenager, still figuring out who I was in His eyes. I thanked Him for this room, for this sacred space, where my past and present could collide in a moment of reflection, of peace. Even here, in the quiet, I knew God's work was still unfolding, and that gave me a deep sense of hope. Opening my eyes, I walked over to the window, my footsteps soft on the creaky floorboards. I reached for the blinds, pulling them open just enough to let the sunlight pour in.

As the darkness of the night filled the room, the chill seemed to lift, just a little. The stillness didn't feel quite as heavy. I smiled softly to myself, feeling a warmth in my chest. Even in a room so long forgotten, I knew that with God, there was always hope for renewal. No matter how broken something seemed, there was always a chance for healing, for something lost to be found again. I could feel it in my heart, this room, this place, could still be restored, just like so many other things in life. I only had to trust in that. I layed back onro my old bed, and smelt the smell I had became used to not many years ago. The smell sent cold chills down my body, as they were not bad chills, but the chills you get when you experience a memory. As I closed my eyes, I felt the embrace of my childhood wrap around me. A little version of me, little

Claire had grown up here. And I missed every second of it.

The next morning, as I drove back to campus, I couldn't stop replaying the weekend in my mind. The warmth of home, the love of my family, and my dad's words, it all filled me with gratitude. I realized how lucky I was to have these moments, to be surrounded by people who loved me unconditionally. Arriving back at my dorm, I stepped into the shower, humming a tune my dad used to sing to me when I was little. The melody brought back memories of bedtime stories and prayers whispered by my bedside. As the warm water washed over me, I felt an overwhelming sense of peace. Not long after, I was drying off, I knelt by my bed, praying for strength, guidance, and gratitude as God had me there for a reason in that moment. I put on some running clothes I had just bought back at home with mom. A really cute pink top that covered from the bottom of my neck, to right below my belly button, and shorts that matched color, that I really loved. After I had got dried off completely, but left my hair down to dry itself.

When I got outside to begin my mile run, the crisp air filled my lungs as I jogged along the path by the quad.

1 mile.

2 miles.

And finally 3 miles.

I was exhausted and decided I was done for the day. I took two steps into my dorm room, and fell into one of the best naps I had ever had.

12

With trust, comes truth.

As Sutton opened up more, I started to see the cracks in his confidence. One night after a long study session, he admitted he often felt like a fraud.

"I'm supposed to have it all together, football, med school, everything. But sometimes, I don't even know if I belong here."

It broke my heart to hear him say that. "Sutton, you're not alone. We all have doubts. But God doesn't call the qualified; He qualifies the called."

He gave me a small, unsure smile. "You really believe that, don't you?"

"With all my heart," I said.

Sutton paused for a long time, his eyes scanning the papers in front of us but clearly lost in thought.

"I guess I've been pretending for so long. I'm not sure who I am anymore," he admitted.

It was the most vulnerable moment I had ever seen from him. I reached across the table and placed my hand over his.

"Sutton, God knows exactly who you are, and He's the one who created you with a purpose."

Time had passed and I found myself praying, I prayed for Sutton again, asking God to show him his worth and help him find his purpose. It was hard to see someone so strong on the outside feel so broken on the inside. But maybe his vulnerability was a sign that he was finally letting down his walls. I could only hope he would find the strength to let God heal those cracks.

The days following our conversation seemed to drag for Sutton. I could see it in his eyes, the weariness that came from balancing football, med school, and the pressure he placed on himself to excel at both. I knew Sutton's passion for football ran deep; it had always been a part of his identity, the thing that defined him. But recently, football had become more of a burden than a joy. He had always pushed through, telling himself that everything would be worth it once he made it. But the stress of the long practices, the expectations from coaches, and the pressure from his teammates was starting to take a toll on him. I could see it in his exhaustion, the way he seemed to drag himself through each day, as if he was carrying a weight heavier than he could bear.

"Claire," Sutton said one afternoon as we sat outside after a long practice, "I don't know how much longer I can keep up with this. I feel like I'm drowning."

His words were like a punch to the gut, a stark contrast to the confident athlete I had first met. I had always admired his resilience, the way he seemed to power through everything, but now I could see the cracks in that armor.

I gently placed my hand on his arm, hoping to offer him some comfort. "You don't have to do this alone, Sutton. You've been carrying so much on your shoulders, and I can see it's wearing you down."

"I just… I can't fail," he confessed, his voice barely above a whisper. "Everyone expects me to be this perfect athlete, this perfect student. But inside, I'm falling apart. I'm terrified that if I let anyone see that, it'll all come crashing down."

I knew Sutton wasn't just talking about football or med school. He was talking about his entire identity, everything he had built his life around. The idea of losing that sense of self terrified him. I could see the way he wrestled with it every day, trying to find balance but feeling like he was being pulled in a thousand different directions.

"You don't have to be perfect," I said softly. "It's okay to not have it all together. God's grace is bigger than any mistake you make. And you don't have to be anyone other than who He's created you to be."

Sutton let out a shaky breath, his shoulders slumping as if some of the weight had been lifted, if only for a moment.

But it wasn't enough. The next few weeks were some of the hardest he had faced. Football season was in full swing, and the demands on Sutton only seemed to increase. He would come to practice exhausted, his mind barely able to focus on the plays, his body too drained to push himself like he used to. The tension in his muscles was constant, a sign that his stress was eating away at him, slowly eroding the person he used to be. I would often find him late at night, sitting in the library or in his dorm room, pouring over notes, trying to catch up on schoolwork that had piled up during the hectic weeks. It was a never-ending cycle, and I could see the toll it was taking on his mental and emotional health.

The smile he once wore so effortlessly was becoming a rare sight. Instead, I saw the lines of worry etched into his face, the deep circles under his eyes from sleepless nights.

"I don't know what to do anymore," Sutton said one evening, his voice trembling with frustration. "I've worked so hard to get here, but I feel like I'm losing literally everything. I don't even know who I'm doing this for anymore."

 I sat beside him, my heart aching for him. "Sutton, maybe you're trying to prove something to everyone except the one person who matters most, God."

His gaze flickered to mine, confusion clouding his eyes. "What do you mean?"

"I mean," I said gently, "you're trying to earn your worth through what you do, not who you are in Christ. Football and med school are great, but they don't define you. You're not a failure if you don't make every pass or ace every exam. God created you with so much more purpose than just that."

He didn't respond right away. For a long time, we sat there in silence, the weight of the truth hanging between us. I knew it wasn't going to be an easy shift for him. But I also knew that God was working in his heart, slowly, gently, leading him toward a deeper understanding of who he was in Christ. In the days that followed, I continued to pray for Sutton, asking God to help him see himself through His eyes. I knew that Sutton's stress and struggles weren't going to disappear overnight, but I also knew that God was with him, even in the hardest moments.

There were days when Sutton seemed to take a step forward, finding a moment of peace in the chaos. Other days, he seemed to spiral deeper into the pressure and stress, questioning everything he had worked for. But through it all, he never stopped seeking God. And that, I realized, was the most important part of his journey. It meant everything to me to see Sutton slowly opening his heart to God. I could see it in the way he spoke about his faith, less defensively, less as something he had to hold on to for appearance's sake. He was beginning to understand that faith wasn't about perfection; it was about trusting in God even when everything felt uncertain. One evening, Sutton asked me to pray with him before practice. It was a simple, sincere prayer, asking God for strength and guidance. But to me, it was a breakthrough. He was no longer pretending to have it all together. He was acknowledging his weaknesses and surrendering them to God.

"I don't know what's ahead, Claire," he said afterward, his voice quiet. "But I'm starting to feel like I don't have to do this alone anymore."

I smiled, my heart full of gratitude. "You never have to do it alone. God's always with you, Sutton."

He nodded, a weight lifting off his shoulders as if the truth had finally sunk in. For the first time in weeks, I saw a glimmer of the Sutton I had known before, strong, but not because he had it all figured out. Strong because he was learning to trust in God, to let go of the need to control everything. The road ahead would still be difficult. There would be struggles, setbacks, and moments of doubt. But as long as Sutton continued to lean on God, I knew he would find his way. And no matter how hard things got, I would be there to remind him that he was never alone. The next few days were tough for him, I could tell. He seemed distracted in class, his mind racing, constantly rehashing the pressures that were slowly suffocating him. One night, after a late study session, Sutton looked like he was about to collapse from exhaustion.

His eyes were bloodshot, and there was a deep weariness in his posture that made my heart ache. I walked beside him as we made our way back to the dorms, knowing that he was barely holding it together.

"You should rest," I suggested. "You're pushing yourself too hard."

He shook his head, but there was no conviction behind it. "I can't afford to rest. There's too much at stake."

I stopped walking, grabbing his arm to get his attention.

"Sutton, you can't keep going like this. You're human, not a machine. You need sleep. You need a break."

He hesitated, then sighed deeply, looking down at the ground. "I know, but if I stop, if I slow down for even a second... I feel like everything will fall apart."

I placed my hand gently on his arm again. "You don't have to do this alone, Sutton. You don't have to carry it all on your own. Let me help."

He looked at me, his face softening.

"I don't know what I'd do without you, Claire. You always know exactly what to say."

"Well, I don't always have the right answers, but I'll be here. You don't have to face this by yourself."

Sutton nodded, looking at me with a gratitude that made my heart flutter.

"Thank you," he whispered, his voice thick with emotion.

I could tell that my words were sinking in, reaching the parts of him that had been locked away for so long.

As we walked the rest of the way back to the dorm, the silence felt different, less heavy, more comforting. I couldn't fix his problems, but I could be there for him. And in that moment, that's all I needed to do. The next week, things didn't magically get better for Sutton, but there were small victories. One afternoon, after an especially difficult practice, Sutton collapsed into one of the chairs in the student lounge, exhausted and visibly defeated.

He looked up at me with a half-smile and shrugged. "Well, I didn't die today. So I guess that's something."

I couldn't help but laugh at his attempt to joke through the exhaustion.

"You're a survivor, Sutton. And you're stronger than you give yourself credit for."

He gave me a tired smile, his eyes softening as he leaned back in the chair.

"I seriously don't know what I'd do without you, Claire. I'm pretty sure I'd have lost my mind by now if it wasn't for you."

I leaned in, teasing. "Well, I do have a way of keeping you grounded. Someone has to keep you from flying off the deep end."

Sutton chuckled, but there was a glimmer of appreciation in his eyes. "You're definitely that person."

In the days that followed, I could see more moments of clarity in him. It wasn't like the pressure disappeared, it was still there, as strong as ever, but he seemed to be facing it with a little more peace. He wasn't pretending anymore, not with me. And that meant everything. One evening, as we sat together in the library, Sutton reached over and took my hand in his. His touch was gentle, tentative, like he was testing the waters. My heart skipped a beat at the unexpected gesture, but I didn't pull away. Instead, I smiled softly, watching him.

"Claire, I don't know what the future holds, but I know one thing for sure, I'm not doing this without you," he said quietly, his voice filled with sincerity.

My heart melted at his words, and I squeezed his hand gently.

"You never have to do it alone. Not as long as I'm here."

And just like that, I realized that no matter what the future held for us, we were walking through it *together*.

The road ahead would still be filled with challenges, but I was starting to see that Sutton was beginning to understand the most important thing of all: he didn't have to have it all figured out. He didn't have to carry the weight of the world on his shoulders. He just had to trust that God would carry him, and that I would be there every step of the way.

As we finished that evening, Sutton's hand lingered a little longer in mine. His gaze met mine, and for the first time in a long while, I saw the hint of peace in his eyes. It wasn't the kind of peace that comes from having everything figured out, it was the kind that comes from surrender. And I couldn't have been more proud of him.

"Goodnight, Claire," Sutton whispered, his voice low and full of meaning. "Thank you. For everything."

I smiled, my heart full of warmth.

"Goodnight, Sutton. I'm always here for you."

13

As the semester pressed on, the weight of my schoolwork began to pile up more, and more.

My calculus midterm, looming deadlines for papers, and group projects were all competing for my attention, making the days feel endless. Yet, despite the stress, I couldn't shake the feeling that prayer was something I could rely on. There were nights I would sit by my window, watching the sunset as I spoke to God, asking Him to help me carry the burdens of the day. Prayer wasn't just for the good times or when things were easy. It was in these moments of stress and exhaustion that I saw its true power, prayer allowed me to surrender everything to God. I could feel God's presence in the little things, the encouragement I received from my professors, the small acts of kindness from strangers, and even the quiet moments of peace during my busy days. I had learned that when I prayed, God would open doors, calm my fears, and give me the strength I needed. And it wasn't always immediate or in the ways I expected, but it was always there. There were days when I felt drained, like there was nothing left to give, but after praying, I found a new sense of purpose.

Sutton had started to open up more, and I could tell that my prayers for him were making a difference. He still had his struggles, but each time we talked, I saw a glimmer of hope in his eyes.

One evening, as we sat in the lounge after dinner, he looked at me and said, "You know, Claire, I think I'm starting to get it. There's more to life than just existing. I've been praying more, and I feel like… I don't know, like something's changing."

I couldn't help but smile, knowing that God was working in his heart. The thought of Christmas was also beginning to take over my mind. With the semester nearing its end, I found myself daydreaming about the upcoming holiday. It wasn't just the break I was looking forward to, it was the chance to spend time with my family, the laughter, the joy of giving, and most of all, the reminder of why we celebrated in the first place. As much as I loved the academic challenges, there was something so refreshing about Christmas. It was a season of hope, of renewal, of remembering the greatest gift we had ever received, the birth of Jesus.

Kelli, my best friend and dorm mate, was just as excited as I was about Christmas. We had been planning together for weeks, thinking about the gifts we wanted to give, the meals we hoped to share, and the traditions we would start. We had decided to decorate our dorm room together, stringing lights across the ceiling and hanging up a small, fake tree by the window. It wasn't much, but it felt like home. I smiled as I watched Kelli hang up a little star ornament we had bought together at a local shop. "This is going to be the best Christmas yet!!" she said, her eyes sparkling with excitement. I couldn't wait to go home for the holidays.

But before I could get there, I had to survive the rest of finals.

The pressure of exams and papers was taking its toll, but every time I felt overwhelmed, I would take a deep breath and pray. I would ask for God's wisdom, His guidance, and His strength to carry me through the final stretch. It wasn't always easy to focus, especially with the Christmas season in full swing, but I knew I had to finish strong.

The thought of pursuing my nursing career was a constant source of motivation. It was my dream, my calling, and I was more determined than ever to make it a reality. I had seen the way nurses could make a difference in people's lives, and it was something I wanted to be a part of. Every prayer I said was filled with gratitude for the opportunity to study, to learn, and to one day help those in need. Nursing wasn't just a career choice; it was a way to serve others, to show them the love of Christ in a tangible way.

I prayed for clarity in my studies, for guidance in choosing the right path, and for the strength to keep going even when it felt like everything was stacked against me. Kelli was equally passionate about her future, though she was still figuring out what path to

take. We spent many nights talking about our hopes,
our dreams, and our struggles.

I could see the doubt in her eyes sometimes, the
uncertainty about what the future held, but I always
reminded her to trust in God's plan.

"You'll get there," I would tell her. "Just keep praying,
keep trusting. God will show you the way."

 I believed that with all my heart. I knew He had big
things in store for both of us. The closer Christmas
came, the more I found myself looking forward to the
break. The idea of taking a breath, of having a moment
to relax and recharge, filled me with excitement. But
even as I anticipated the joy of Christmas, I felt an
overwhelming sense of peace in my heart, knowing
that no matter how stressful school or life got, I had
the power of prayer to lean on. I had the strength of my
faith, and that was enough. I had spent hours praying
for my family, friends, and even for people I hadn't yet
met. I prayed for the hurting, for the lost, and for those
who didn't know the love of Christ.

I prayed for Sutton, for his healing, and for his
continued growth in faith. I prayed for Kelli, that she
would find the path that was meant for her and that she
would feel the warmth of God's love. I prayed for
myself, for the courage to continue pursuing my
dreams and the wisdom to handle everything life threw
my way.

And as the semester finally came to a close, I felt a
sense of relief wash over me. I had made it through.

Finals were *OVER*!!

The stress was behind me, and Christmas was right around the corner. I was looking forward to the chance to rest, to spend time with my loved ones, and to give thanks for all that God had done. The gift of prayer, the gift of His love, and the gift of family and friendship, these were the things I cherished most. The power of prayer had carried me through one of the busiest and most challenging semesters of my life. It had been my anchor, my source of strength, and my constant reminder that I was never alone.

As I prepared for Christmas with Kelli and looked forward to the new year, I couldn't help but feel grateful for all that God had done in my life. There was so much more ahead, and I knew that no matter where my journey took me, prayer would always be my guiding light.

Christmas drew closer and closer, I found myself praying even more earnestly for Sutton.

I knew he had been wrestling with a lot, but I could sense that the foundation was starting to form. It wasn't about him suddenly having all the answers, but about him beginning to open his heart and mind to the possibility that there was more to life than what he had known. I couldn't help but reflect on how far he had come from the first time we'd spoken about faith. It wasn't an easy road for him, and I knew that, but I trusted that God was working in ways I couldn't fully see.

I prayed that this Christmas, Sutton would encounter the love of Jesus in a deeper way. I prayed that amidst the busy holiday season, with all its distractions, he would have a moment of clarity, where he truly understood the magnitude of what Christmas meant. I prayed that he would come to realize that the greatest gift wasn't something that could be bought or wrapped, but the eternal gift of grace that Jesus offers to each of us. My prayer was simple but filled with hope: that Sutton would find peace, that he would know the joy of God's love, and that this Christmas would be a turning point for him in his relationship with Christ.

That night, as I sat in the quiet of my dorm room, I prayed specifically for Sutton. I asked God to help him see the true meaning of Christmas, not just the presents, the lights, or the festive traditions, but the reason for the season: the birth of Jesus. I prayed that Sutton would come to know that the greatest gift of all wasn't something wrapped under a tree, but the gift of salvation, the gift of Christ's love and sacrifice. I prayed that he would feel the warmth of God's presence in his life and that this Christmas would be a turning point for him, a moment where he truly understood what it meant to be loved by the Savior. It was my deepest hope that Sutton would come to know the peace that only Jesus could give, especially during this season of hope and renewal.

I found myself feeling a blend of exhaustion and anticipation. The thought that I had pushed through the most challenging weeks of school and had come out on the other side, ready for the peace and joy that

Christmas promised. I couldn't help but feel grateful for the way God had carried me through it all, but there was still a part of me that felt like something was missing. I kept thinking about Sutton and the changes I had seen in him, both the struggles and the moments of breakthrough. The thought of him made my heart ache in the best way, like a prayer answered, even though I didn't know what exactly I was praying for.

 One afternoon, as we sat on the steps of the library after a long day, Sutton leaned in a little closer, his voice low and sincere.

"You know, Claire, you've been such a big part of all this. I don't know how I would've gotten through these past few months without you," he said.

I smiled softly, feeling the warmth of his words in my heart.

"You've been pretty amazing yourself, Sutton," I replied, feeling a slight blush on my cheeks.

There was always something about the way he looked at me that made my heart flutter. His dark eyes, full of meaning, held me in place, as if he were waiting for something more, something unspoken. He chuckled, brushing his hand through his hair.

"I don't know about that. I'm still trying to figure things out, but having you around makes it a little easier to keep going."

There was something in his tone that made my breath catch in my throat. As much as I wanted to be strong for him, I could feel the pull between us growing stronger. There was this electricity in the air, a connection that felt undeniable. It wasn't just the vulnerability that Sutton had begun to share with me, it was the way he made me feel like I mattered. As the conversation shifted to Christmas plans, I caught Sutton glancing at me with a playful smile.

"So, are you going to spoil me with some Christmas gifts, or do I have to wait until next year to see what you got me?" he teased, nudging me with his elbow.

I grinned, feeling the heat of the moment. "Oh, trust me," I replied with a teasing smile, "the gifts I'm giving you are worth the wait."

My words hung in the air, and Sutton's gaze softened, almost like he was holding his breath. I had always known Sutton was charming, but in that moment, I realized just how much he could make me feel seen, and not just as a friend.

Later that night, as I sat alone in my dorm room, I replayed our conversation over and over in my mind. His words, the way he had looked at me, and that undeniable chemistry we shared. My heart raced a little faster, and I couldn't help but feel that familiar warmth spread through me whenever Sutton was near. It wasn't just attraction, it was deeper than that. I was beginning to realize that, even though our paths had been different, our hearts were more aligned than I could have ever imagined.

But even as my thoughts wandered, I knew I couldn't let myself get lost in the idea of us just yet. My faith, my calling as a NICU nurse, and my future were too important to let anything distract me. Still, as Christmas drew closer and the days grew colder, I found myself praying not only for guidance but also for clarity when it came to Sutton. What did God have in store for the two of us? And if we were to grow closer, how would that fit into His plan?

14

Semesters, months, weeks, and days passed, and passed, Sutton and I grew closer than little me would have ever imagined.

Our friendship deepened in ways I hadn't imagined. I had always been the one to support others, but now, I felt the same sense of being supported by him. I began to see him not just as someone I was helping, but as a true friend who was helping me too. Every time I struggled with school work, Sutton was there. I couldn't shake the feeling that something important was happening, that the space between Sutton and me had shifted in a way I hadn't expected. Every text message he sent, every word he spoke, seemed to carry more weight than before. He wasn't just the person I'd grown close to during our time at UNC, he was becoming something more. And yet, there were still so many uncertainties, so many questions that hung in the air between us. I didn't know where this was leading, but I couldn't deny that a part of me hoped it would lead to something deeper. He'd sit beside me as I buried myself in textbooks, offering encouragement when I felt overwhelmed. And when I cheered him on at football games, I noticed his smile was brighter. It meant something to him that I was there, and that meant everything to me. Sutton had always had his own battles, but in the past few months, I could see him starting to soften.

He would ask how my day was going, offering support even when it wasn't needed. I began to realize that his presence wasn't just a coincidence, it was an indication of the way we had become intertwined in each other's lives. I showed up for him at every game, cheering loudly from the stands, and in return, Sutton made sure I was never alone when the weight of school became too much. His voice was always the one I heard, grounding me when I felt myself slipping. But there was something more growing between us, something deeper than simple friendship. We both noticed it, though we never spoke about it directly. Our bond was built on kindness, support, and shared moments, yet we both knew that what was happening between us couldn't be categorized so easily.

Another day as we sat together in the library, Sutton leaned over and whispered, "I'm proud of you, Claire. I know this semester has been tough, but you're getting through it." He smiled, and it made my heart flutter once again.

I had always admired Sutton, but this was different. There was more affection behind his words than just friendship. I found myself wishing I could tell him how I felt. But I held back, not wanting to complicate things. Over the next few weeks, Sutton and I continued to grow closer, though it wasn't always easy.

As much as I tried to help him with his academic struggles and personal battles, I began to realize there was a side to him that he kept hidden. His vulnerability was starting to show through the cracks, but he wasn't always willing to talk about it. Still, I didn't push him. Instead, I tried to be a steady presence in his life, offering encouragement and prayer, trusting that he would come to me when he was ready. There were moments when I could tell he was trying to open up, but he'd retreat just as quickly. It wasn't that he didn't trust me; it was that the weight of his past, especially his relationship with Maggie, had left deep scars.

Our connection deepened over shared moments of quiet support. I had been there for Sutton through the stress of his classes and the exhaustion from football practice. I was one of the few people who truly understood the pressures he faced, and in a way, I think that made him feel safe around me. But what I didn't know was that Sutton was struggling with something much deeper than I realized. As much as I tried to be there for him, there were still pieces of his past that haunted him, pieces he hadn't yet learned to let go of. I could sense the heaviness in his voice sometimes when he spoke about his past with Maggie.

I knew there was a story there that needed to be shared, but Sutton wasn't ready to tell it, and I wasn't going to push him. Even though he wasn't fully open about everything, our friendship continued to blossom. I attended every football game, cheering him on from the stands, and in return, Sutton was there for me when I needed a little encouragement or support with my schoolwork. His encouragement was always so genuine. He would sit beside me in the library for hours, helping me study, offering tips on how to manage my time better, and keeping my spirits up when I started to feel overwhelmed by exams. It was in those quiet moments, studying side by side, that I felt a sense of calm and comfort, knowing we were growing not just as friends, but as something more. Every gesture, every word of encouragement from him, made me feel seen, as if I were truly important to him in a way I couldn't yet define. But deep inside, I had to acknowledge that something had shifted between us. The friendship was no longer just about mutual respect and support, it had become something more tender, something that tugged at my heart in ways I wasn't prepared for. It was a slow evolution, but there was a gentle intimacy that developed over time.

His presence made me feel *safe*, and I began to realize that I looked forward to our time together more than I wanted to admit.

However, with that realization came a fear of complicating things. I cared deeply for Sutton, and I could sense that his feelings for me were becoming something more than just platonic, too. But we both avoided talking about it, not wanting to risk disrupting the fragile balance we had worked so hard to build.

Then one night, as we sat together in my dorm room, Sutton was helping me prepare for an upcoming test. He was patient, guiding me through the material with the same care he had shown on the football field. Just as I was beginning to relax, his phone rang. He glanced at it and excused himself, stepping into the hallway to take the call. I sat there, my mind still on our conversation, when I heard Sutton's voice rise in frustration. The tone was sharp, filled with a mix of disbelief and anger. Curious, I stood and walked over to the door, leaning against the frame.

"Why are you posting all those pictures, Sutton?! What is this with you and Claire?! You've already moved on?!" Sutton's ex girlfriend Maggie's voice crackled through the phone, venomous and sharp.

Sutton's response was measured, but I could hear the tension in his voice. "Maggie, they're just pictures from a football game. Claire's a friend. You know that."

But Maggie wasn't having it.

"Oh, really? Just a friend? Because it sure doesn't look like that, Sutton. What's all this, huh? You think I'm stupid? Everyone's seeing it. Don't you realize what you've done. You have broken me and you dont even care!?"

I could hear the sound of Maggie's heavy breathing through the phone, her words growing more frantic.

"You were supposed to be mine. You said we'd be together. You can't just move on like this, Sutton. You never should've left me."

Suddenly, there was silence, and I saw Sutton's face pale as he checked his phone. His eyes widened, and he staggered backward, clearly shocked.

He looked up, his voice faltering. "Maggie... what did you do?" Maggie's laughter rang in his ear.

"You should've stayed with me. Maybe we could've prevented all this. Check Instagram. You'll see."

Sutton didn't hesitate, pulling up his social media feed. I grabbed my phone from my pocket, and My heart sank as I saw the hateful comments and explicit photos, images twisted and edited to look like they were taken during moments I knew to be completely innocent.

The things people were saying about him were disgusting, and I could see the toll it was taking on him. His hands trembled as he scrolled through the posts, each one a deeper cut than the last. Maggie had made sure the damage was done.

"Shouldn't have left. We was quite the perfect couple." Maggie said before hanging up.

Sutton stood *frozen*, his face pale with disbelief. He let out a shaky breath, and tears welled up in his eyes.

I took a step forward, instinctively wanting to comfort him, but before I could say anything, Sutton turned toward me. His eyes were filled with anger, hurt, and confusion.

"Look what you've done!" he yelled, his voice raw and shaking. "I told you to stay away from me, Claire. See what you have caused me?!? Why did you have to get involved in all of this? I told you, this would happen. You don't know what it's like to deal with someone like Maggie. Now look at me!?"

My chest tightened as his words hit me like a punch. I couldn't believe what was happening.

This wasn't the Sutton I had come to know, the one who cared so deeply and was always there for me. This was someone I didn't recognize. He stormed out of my dorm, slamming the door behind him. I stood there, frozen, my mind racing.

What had just happened?

Sutton was always so calm, so in control. But now, everything had shifted.I stood there, the weight of Sutton's words still hanging in the air like a dark cloud. My heart pounded in my chest, and for the first time, I felt a deep sense of uncertainty between us. Sutton had always been someone I could rely on, someone who had supported me through my struggles.

And now, in this moment, everything felt like it was falling apart. I didn't know what to do, how to fix it, or even if it was fixable. All I could do was stand there, trying to process what had just transpired, and trying to hold on to the hope that this wasn't the end of everything we had shared. The minutes passed like hours, and as the silence in my dorm room grew heavier, I found myself pacing, my mind racing in a hundred different directions. Why had Sutton reacted like that? Why had he blamed me for what Maggie had done? I could feel the anger and hurt bubbling up inside me, but I knew that confronting him in that moment wasn't the answer. He needed time, time to sort through his feelings, time to face the mess Maggie had created.

But I also knew that this wasn't something that could be swept under the rug. Something had shifted between us, and it was clear that it wasn't just a misunderstanding, it was deeper than that. I grabbed my phone, scrolling through the social media posts that Sutton had seen earlier. The hatred in the comments, the cruel words that people were spewing, made my stomach turn. It wasn't just the pictures Maggie had manipulated; it was everything she had done to tear him apart.

 I couldn't understand why someone would want to destroy Sutton like that.

He didn't deserve it, not the hate, not the lies, not the manipulation. And yet, here we were, caught in the fallout of her actions. My heart ached for him, but I also felt this overwhelming need to protect him, to somehow shield him from the ugliness that had entered our lives. I sent Sutton a text, though I wasn't sure if he would even respond. "I'm here for you, Sutton. Whenever you're ready, we can talk. But I need you to know that none of this is your fault. You're not alone in this." My hands trembled as I hit send, but I hoped that maybe, just maybe, it would reach him. I wasn't sure how much time it would take, but I knew that I couldn't give up on him, not after everything we had been through together. I thought about how much Sutton had opened up to me, how much we had shared. I thought about the tenderness in his words when he told me he was proud of me.

That was the Sutton I knew, the one who cared, who was still so full of potential, despite all the darkness in his past. I wasn't ready to give up on that version of him. And deep down, I believed that he wasn't ready to give up on me either. I couldn't control the actions of others, but I could control how I responded to the situation. I wasn't going to run away or shut myself off from him. I was going to be there, even if it meant taking a step back and giving him the space he needed. Whatever this was between us, whatever we were becoming, it was still worth fighting for. Sutton had a lot of healing left to do, and I wasn't about to leave him to do it alone. I wasn't sure what the future held, but I knew one thing for sure: I was going to stand by him, no matter what. I wanted to go after him, to explain, but I knew he wasn't ready to hear anything I had to say.

 He was in so much pain, and I didn't know how to fix *us*.

15

When the door slammed behind Sutton, and I just stood there, in shock.

A cold lump of confusion settling in my stomach. His words echoed in my mind, each one sharper than the last.

"Look what you've done!" "Why did you have to get involved?"

I could still hear the tremor in his voice, the pain cutting through the anger. I knew Maggie wasn't an easy person to deal with. She had always been a shadow in the background of Sutton's life, lingering and controlling in ways I couldn't fully understand. But what had just happened felt like a storm had torn through the fragile space we had built between us.

What had I done? All I'd ever wanted was to be there for him, to offer support and encouragement. Yet somehow, my presence had sparked this painful eruption. The anger in his eyes, the bitterness in his words, this was not the Sutton I knew. I didn't want to believe that I was the cause of his turmoil. Maggie's grip on him had always been strong, but I'd never imagined it would come to this, not when he'd started to lean on me. It was as if, in her eyes, I was the one to blame for everything that went wrong. But I hadn't asked for any of this. I sank down onto the edge of my bed, my hands trembling.

The images, the comments, my mind kept flashing back to the screen, to the cruel things people had said. The thought of Sutton being torn apart like that made me want to scream. But there was nothing I could do to take away the pain, no quick fix. I didn't even know where to start. I reached for my phone, trying to process everything. I wanted to reach out to him, to send a message, but I couldn't find the right words. How could I make him understand that I hadn't meant for any of this to happen? But he didn't want to hear it. Not now, anyway.

After what felt like hours, I finally stood and grabbed my jacket.

I didn't know where I was going, but I couldn't sit still any longer. Sutton needed space, but he also needed to know that I wasn't going anywhere. I wasn't going to let him push me away. I wandered through campus, the cold air biting at my cheeks as I tried to clear my head.

Every step felt heavier than the last, as if the weight of everything that had happened hung over me. Sutton wasn't just a friend anymore. He had become something more, something I wasn't sure how to define. And now, with Maggie's chaos in the mix, I was afraid that we might not make it out of this intact.

I found myself outside the library, standing near the bench where Sutton and I had sat countless times, studying and talking about everything and nothing. I had hoped for a calm moment, for things to just fall into place.

Instead, it felt like the world was unraveling faster than I could catch up.

My phone buzzed in my pocket, and my heart skipped a beat. It was a message from Kelli. *"You okay? I heard what happened. Let me know if you need me."*

I stared at the screen, my fingers hovering over the keys. *How could I explain this to her?* I thought. She was one of the few people who truly understood the bond Sutton and I had built, but she didn't know the whole story. Not the part about Maggie, not the part about how I was starting to feel something more than friendship.

I quickly typed back, *"I don't know what just happened. Everything's a mess right now. I just need some time to think."*

I didn't feel like talking. Not yet. I wasn't even sure what to say, what to do next. It was all too raw, too painful to process in that moment. Then, a sound broke through my thoughts, footsteps.

A figure approached from the distance, and I turned to see Sutton walking toward me, his eyes red, his face drawn in a way I had never seen before. He looked like he hadn't slept, like the weight of the world had been dropped on him and he was struggling to carry it alone. I froze, unsure of what to do. He had come to me, but what could I say? What could we say to each other after everything that had happened? He stopped a few feet away, his gaze avoiding mine, as though he couldn't bear to look me in the eyes.

The silence between us stretched on, thick and heavy, before he finally spoke.

"I'm sorry," he muttered, his voice low and broken. "I shouldn't have yelled at you. I'm just," He paused, clenching his fists. "I don't know what to do anymore."

I wanted to run to him, to tell him everything would be okay. But I knew I couldn't promise that. Not now.

"It's not your fault," I said softly, my voice shaking. "You're hurting, and I get that. I just want to help you, Sutton. I don't know what to say or do, but I'm here for you. I always will be."

He looked up at me then, his eyes full of pain and regret. For a moment, neither of us moved, just standing there, caught in the tangled emotions that had defined so much of our time together. "I don't want you to get hurt because of me," he whispered, his voice thick with vulnerability.

"Maggie… she's not done with me. She'll never be done."

I stepped forward, closing the gap between us. "And I'll be right here, standing by you, through it all."

Sutton didn't say anything for a moment, his eyes searching mine, as if trying to decide if he could trust me with everything. The weight of his past, his pain, it was all there, just below the surface. And in that silence, I knew we were both trying to figure out how to move forward, how to turn this tangled mess into something that might one day heal. I wasn't sure if we could fix everything overnight.

But I knew one thing for certain: I wasn't going anywhere. Not now. Not ever. Sutton's lips parted as if to say something, but before the words could come, we were interrupted by a voice behind us.

"Claire?" I turned, seeing Kelli standing there, her face full of concern.

I wasn't sure how long she had been watching us, but I didn't care. Right now, I needed her more than I had ever realized.

" I think we could all use a little space," she said gently.

I nodded, my chest tight, and for the first time in what felt like forever, I let myself breathe. As Kelli walked up to us, her presence seemed to break the tension, giving us both a little room to breathe. She looked between me and Sutton, her eyes soft with little understanding but filled with the sharp awareness of the situation.

She knew something was off, but I could see that she didn't want to press. Kelli was always good at reading people, knowing when to give them space and when to step in. "I think we could all use a little space," she repeated herself again, her tone calm yet insistent.

"Let's grab a coffee, Claire. You look like you could use a break."

I hesitated for a moment, but I could feel the weight of Sutton's pain still hanging in the air, an unspoken understanding between us. He needed time to process, just as I did. Maybe this was the pause we both needed to clear our heads before we said anything more.

"Yeah," I said, nodding, my voice barely above a whisper.

I turned to Sutton, offering him a small, uncertain smile. "I'll… I'll talk to you soon, okay?"

He nodded slowly, his expression unreadable, and for a second, I could see that he was caught between wanting to pull me closer and pushing me away. The pull of his vulnerability was palpable, but so was the fear. His fear of pulling me into his mess, of letting anyone get too close. I walked away with Kelli, my thoughts a swirling storm of emotions.

As we crossed the campus, Kelli didn't ask any questions, she just stayed close, her presence a quiet support. I was grateful for that. There were moments when I needed someone who didn't ask for explanations, someone who just knew. We reached the coffee shop, and I sank into one of the chairs by the window. The warm, earthy aroma of coffee filled the air, but I couldn't focus on it. My mind kept drifting back to Sutton. To the way his voice had cracked when he'd spoken to me, to the pain I saw in his eyes. I felt like I was standing at the edge of something, and I wasn't sure if I should jump or if I should just wait and let the storm pass. Kelli sat down across from me, her eyes gentle but knowing. She didn't have to say much; I could tell she understood that I was struggling to make sense of everything.

"Talk to me, Claire," she said quietly, leaning forward, her voice soft but insistent.

"What happened with Sutton?" I took a deep breath, my fingers tracing the edge of my cup. The truth was, I wasn't sure how to explain. How could I? How could I put into words the mess that had unfolded between us?

"I think I pushed him too hard," I began slowly, my voice barely audible. "I didn't know things were still so complicated with Maggie. I thought we were… I thought we were getting closer. But I didn't realize that being there for him, showing up at the games, even just helping him with school… it stirred up all of these old feelings. And I didn't know how to handle it."

Kelli nodded, her expression softening.

 "It sounds like you're both in a really tough spot. You're not the one to blame for Maggie's actions, Claire. Sutton has his own journey, and sometimes people get tangled up in things they can't control."

I wanted to believe that, but part of me still felt like I had somehow played a role in what had happened. I had gotten too close, too involved, and now Sutton was pulling away from me. There was a rawness in the way he'd spoken to me, like he didn't trust himself, or me, enough to let me help him anymore.

"I don't want to lose him, Kelli," I confessed, my voice shaking a little. "But I don't know if I can keep doing this, not when it feels like every time I get close, something pulls us apart. I'm scared that we've already crossed a line, that maybe we can't go back to being just friends after this."

Kelli reached across the table, placing a hand over mine. Her grip was warm, steady.

"You don't have to have all the answers right now, Claire. And I know it hurts, but sometimes space is what people need. Maybe Sutton needs time to sort through everything. And if you really care about him, then you'll give him that space. He'll come back to you when he's ready. But you can't force it."

I nodded slowly, trying to take in what she was saying. I knew she was right. As much as I wanted to fix things right away, some things couldn't be rushed. Sutton had to deal with his past, with the lingering shadow of Maggie and the mess she had created. And I had to learn how to give him the time he needed, without pushing him into a corner.

"Thanks, Kelli," I said quietly, grateful for her understanding. "I don't know what I'd do without you."

Kelli smiled, squeezing my hand before pulling back. "You'd be just fine. But I'm glad I'm here for you, Claire. And if you ever need to talk, you know I'm always ready to listen."

We sat in silence for a while, sipping our coffee, letting the moment settle between us. I couldn't fix things with Sutton in that moment, but I knew I would be there when he was ready. I just had to trust that he would find his way back to me, that our bond, whatever it was, was strong enough to withstand the storm that had come between us.

Later that night, as I sat in my dorm room, the weight of everything seemed a little less heavy. I still didn't have the answers I was looking for, and I didn't know what tomorrow would bring, but I knew one thing: I wasn't giving up on Sutton. He needed time, and I was willing to wait for him to come back to me. We would find our way through this. Together. The only thing I could do now was pray. And I did, with every ounce of hope I had left, that somehow, Sutton would find the peace he was searching for, and that maybe, just maybe, he would let me be part of that journey.

That was the first time I had ever gotten a text from Sutton Adams.

My phone buzzed late that night, the vibration pulling me out of my thoughts. I glanced down, expecting to see a message from Kelli or maybe a reminder for an assignment. But the name on the screen made my heart skip a beat.

Sutton Adams: "Hey, Claire. I've been thinking about everything. I'm sorry for how I reacted earlier. I was hurt, and I let that get in the way of what's important. I don't know what to say, but I hope you know that I never meant to push you away."

The message sat there for a few seconds, and I had to read it again, just to make sure it was real. The words settled into my chest like a promise. I couldn't say what would happen between us, but in that moment, I knew that whatever came next, we would face it together. And that was more than enough for me. Sutton had never sent me a message like that before. His words were raw, almost fragile. I could feel the sincerity behind each one, and it made my heart ache in a way I hadn't expected.

Claire: "I don't blame you for how you reacted"

I hit send and immediately regretted not waiting longer.

Sutton Adams: "I don't know how you do it. I've been through a lot, and I never really let anyone in. But you, every time I start to push you away, you're right there, staying by my side. I don't deserve that. I don't know how to explain it, but I'm grateful for you."

I read the text over and over again, feeling a mix of relief and confusion. He had a way of making me feel important, even when he was struggling with so much. It was like he saw something in me that no one else had. But his words also made me nervous. I wasn't sure what this meant for us, or what it meant for him.

Claire: "You don't need to apologize, Sutton. I just want you to be okay. I know you've been through a lot with Maggie and everything, and I can't imagine how hard that is. But you don't have to carry it alone."

I paused, unsure of whether I should add more. I wanted to remind him that I was here for him, but I didn't want to overwhelm him.

A moment later, Sutton responded, his words slow but thoughtful.

Sutton Adams: "I don't know if I'm ready to talk about it all. But I do know that you've made me feel less alone, even when I didn't deserve it. Thank you for not giving up on me. I don't know where this goes, or what happens next, but I want you to know that you matter."

I stared at the text for a long time. My hands were trembling slightly as I typed back.

Claire: "You matter too, Sutton. And I'm not going anywhere."

There was a long pause before he replied again. This time, his message was shorter, but it carried a weight I hadn't expected.

Sutton Adams: "I'm not sure what happens next either. But I don't want to lose you."

My heart swelled at his words. I had been so afraid of pushing him too far, of complicating things further. But here we were, acknowledging the shift between us, the bond that had grown in silence and shared moments.

Claire: "You won't lose me. I promise."

After that, there was a quiet calm that settled between us. No more texts came that night, but I knew that something had shifted. There was a crack in the wall Sutton had built around himself, and maybe, just maybe, it was wide enough for me to fit into. I didn't know where this would lead, but for the first time in a long while, I felt like we were on the same page. It was a small step forward, but it was progress. And in that moment, that was enough.

As I sat there, staring at my phone, my heart was full of so many conflicting emotions. Relief and anxiety fought for dominance, but underneath it all, there was a quiet hope that hadn't been there before. Sutton's words had pierced through the wall of silence we had been living in for so long. I had been afraid of what this would mean for us, whether we were on the brink of something deeper, or if the pain from Maggie's shadow would drive us apart for good. But now, I could feel that we were both standing on the same fragile ground, trying to rebuild the trust that had been broken. I couldn't say where this journey would take us, but I knew that I wasn't ready to walk away. The night stretched on, and I found myself replaying our conversation over and over again. Sutton had always been guarded, a master at keeping his emotions buried beneath layers of sarcasm and humor. But tonight, he had peeled back some of that armor, revealing glimpses of the person he truly was, the person who had been hurt so deeply by Maggie, the person who had learned to protect himself at all costs. I wanted to reach through the phone and hold him, to offer comfort in the way that I knew how. But there was nothing more I could do right now. He had already taken a huge step by opening up, even if it was only a small one. I couldn't push him for more. Not yet. I sighed and set my phone down on the table beside me, my mind still tangled in thoughts of Sutton. It felt like we had been here before, standing at the edge of something we weren't sure how to navigate.

There had always been this unspoken connection between us, something deeper than friendship, but we had never acknowledged it, at least, not fully. And now, with everything that had happened, I wasn't sure what to make of it. Was this just a moment of vulnerability, a crack in the walls that would eventually close? Or was this the beginning of something new, something that could withstand the pressures of the past? I couldn't know for sure. All I could do was be patient, be there for him in whatever way he needed me, and let time reveal what came next.

As the hours passed and I finally laid my head down on my pillow, I found myself praying again. The words came as easily as they always did, but tonight, there was something different about my prayer. I wasn't asking for Sutton to change or for things to magically fix themselves. Instead, I asked for strength, for him, for me, for both of us. I asked for peace, for clarity in the midst of all the uncertainty. I prayed that Sutton would be able to find healing, and that somehow, our bond would become stronger as a result of the struggles we had faced. And most of all, I prayed that I wouldn't lose my way in the process. It was so easy to get caught up in the chaos of it all, to lose sight of the things that truly mattered. But I didn't want to lose myself. Not in this, not in Sutton's pain, not in anything.

When I woke up the next morning, the weight of everything still lingered. I couldn't shake the feeling that things had changed, like we had crossed some invisible line, and now there was no going back. But there was also something reassuring about it. It was a new beginning, of sorts, and though it was uncertain, it was ours. I had to remind myself that this wasn't going to be easy. Sutton had so much to work through, and I couldn't rush him. But in that moment, I knew I was willing to wait. He had already shown me more of himself than I ever thought he would, and that was enough to keep me going. If I had to give him space to heal, then I would. But I wouldn't give up on him. Later that morning, I met Kelli for breakfast, and the conversation turned to Sutton almost immediately. Kelli could always tell when something was off, and she didn't shy away from asking questions.

But today, there was a softness to her approach, an understanding that I hadn't seen before.

"How are you doing?" she asked gently, her eyes filled with concern.

I paused, taking a deep breath before answering. "I'm okay. I think."

It felt like a half-truth, but I didn't want to burden her with all the things I was still processing.

"I just don't know what to expect anymore. Everything with Sutton is… different now. And I'm trying to figure out what that means for us."

Kelli nodded, her expression thoughtful. "You don't have to figure it all out at once, Claire. You're both in a really messy situation, and it's okay to not have the answers right away. Just take it one step at a time, and trust that things will work out. Whatever happens, you've already shown Sutton that you care, and that means more than you might realize."

Her words were a balm to my restless heart, and I realized she was right. There was no rush. I didn't have to have it all figured out.

All I could do was continue showing up, continue being there for him, and let things unfold as they would. As the days passed, I did my best to stay grounded. I focused on my schoolwork, spending time with Kelli, and trying not to overthink everything. But in the back of my mind, I couldn't help but wonder when Sutton would be ready to talk more. Would he reach out again? Would he be able to share more about what he had been through with Maggie, or would he keep it all locked away? I didn't know, but I promised myself I wouldn't push him. I had learned that much by now. Sometimes, the best way to love someone was to let them come to you when they were ready.

And I was willing to wait. The following week, I saw Sutton again, briefly, in passing, on campus. He didn't say much, but there was a softness in his eyes, a quiet acknowledgment of the space between us that had been filled with unspoken words. We exchanged a look, a brief smile, and that was enough. It was the first time since the argument that I felt like we were in the same place again, even if it was only for a moment. Maybe we were both still figuring things out, but I had hope. And hope was a powerful thing.

All that mattered was we was on good terms, and God was in control.

16

My mind is *spinning*.

Fortunately, I had prayed so hard, I overcome the care of Sutton's ignorance after a couple of days pass by, and Sutton and I conclude we are going to meet up at the local coffee shop after classes. As I am walking in, my eyes are drawn straight to Sutton, sitting in the corner of the coffee shop, flowers in hand and his smile as big as I could ever describe.

I approached him in shock, and confusion, as he hugs me I feel my heart get this feeling I only felt when I was hugged by a family member, or a closest friend I could imagine. I noticed Sutton has something in his hand, when all of a sudden Sutton says,

"I wrote you something Claire." Oh, and you look beautiful."

"Thank you, Sutton." I said as I was reaching for the envelope in his hand.

When Sutton handed me the letter, my hands shook ever so slightly as I took it from him. I could feel the weight of it, both physically and emotionally, in the way it rested in my palms.

As I unfolded the paper, I braced myself for the words that would follow, not knowing what to expect. I started reading each sentence with care, letting his thoughts sink in one by one.

The honesty in his words felt like a revelation, a glimpse into the vulnerability he had kept hidden for so long. His letter wasn't just an expression of thanks, as it read:

"Dear Claire, I've never been good at expressing myself in words, but I feel like I need to try, at least this once. I've spent a long time keeping my feelings and thoughts locked up, afraid of letting anyone see what's really inside. But you've shown me something different, something better. From the moment we met, you've been there for me. You've been patient, kind, and steady, even when I didn't deserve it. You've supported me when I didn't know how to support myself, and you've helped me believe in the possibility of change. For that, I'll always be grateful. I know I've kept parts of myself hidden from you, parts that I'm not proud of, but you've never once pushed me to share. You've accepted me where I was and given me space to grow. I don't know if I'll ever be able to fully express what that means to me, but I hope this letter is a step toward showing you how much I appreciate you. I want you to know that the more time I spend with you, the more I realize how much I care for you. I've been

holding back, afraid of making things complicated or risking what we've built. But I don't want to keep pretending anymore. I'm not sure where all this is going, but I know I want to explore it with you, as long as you're willing to. You mean more to me than I ever thought anyone could. Thank you for being you, for being my friend, my support, and my peace in the chaos. I hope this letter shows you even a fraction of what I feel. You've changed my life, and I'll never take that for granted.

-Sincerely, Sutton"

It was an invitation into a deeper understanding for both of us, a space where our connection could *grow*.

I had always paid close attention to the smallest details, a habit that came naturally to me. I noticed the little things in people, an expression that lingered just a second too long, the way someone's voice trembled when they were about to say something important, or the way someone's eyes brightened when they talked about something they loved. In my prayers, I often asked God to give me the eyes to see what others couldn't, to help me understand what people were going through even when they didn't say a word.

This was the gift I'd been given, and I saw it as a responsibility, a way to care for others in a world that was often too busy to notice the silent struggles around them. I loved deeply, often without expectation. It wasn't just my closest friends who felt the impact of my heart, but even the strangers I passed by every day. I never knew their stories, but somehow, I felt a deep compassion for them, for their unspoken battles. That night, as I read Sutton's letter, I whispered a prayer of gratitude for the people I loved and for those whose paths had crossed mine in fleeting ways. I prayed for understanding and strength for all of us, knowing that even the most seemingly insignificant encounters could shape lives in ways we couldn't always comprehend.

Sutton's words were a reflection of what had happened not only between us but inside of him, too, a change I could sense but had never fully understood until now. I could feel the weight of Sutton's past in every word he wrote. His letter spoke of the struggle he had faced, both internally and with others, but it also held a thread of hope, the possibility of something new.

 He acknowledged how I had stood by him, how I had never let go, even when he was pushing everyone away. His gratitude was real, but it was more than that, he was offering me something vulnerable, something precious. He wasn't just thanking me; he was showing me a piece of his soul that I hadn't seen before, one that had been locked away for far too long. Sutton had always been someone who carried a weight, a heaviness I could see but could never fully understand. His relationship with Maggie had left scars, deep ones, and it was clear that it wasn't just a past that haunted him, it was a present that still affected him, in ways he couldn't yet express. But here, in the letter, he had done what I hadn't expected, he had let me in. He had opened up in a way that was so completely different from the way he had been before. This was the Sutton I had always believed in, the one who could be brave enough to confront his past, to acknowledge the impact of it, and to trust someone else to be there for him. I finished reading the letter, my heart swelling with emotion. It was a small act, but one that carried such weight.

I understood now, this wasn't just a simple thank-you. It was a beginning. A start to something deeper, something more genuine, something that had the potential to heal the parts of us that needed it the most. But I also knew that healing wouldn't be easy. The road ahead would be long, and we would both have to walk it carefully, side by side. I held the letter to my chest for a moment, closing my eyes as I let the weight of it settle in my heart.

I could feel the connection between us growing, not just in the shared moments we had but in the understanding that was beginning to take root. This wasn't the end of our story, it was just the beginning of something that was still unfolding, like a delicate flower slowly opening to the sun. I whispered another prayer then, asking for strength, for Sutton, and for me. I prayed that his journey of healing would continue, and that I would be there for him, as I had promised. I asked for guidance, for clarity in knowing how best to support him as he navigated the complexities of his past and the uncertainty of his future. And above all, I prayed for patience, patience to wait for the answers that would come in time, knowing that we didn't need to rush this process. I placed the letter on my desk, my mind racing with all the thoughts that swirled around my head.

Sutton had reached out to me in a way I hadn't expected, and I felt the weight of it settle in my chest. But I wasn't afraid of what it meant. I had always believed in the power of connection, in the way two people could change each other's lives if they were willing to be vulnerable. And Sutton had just shown me that he was willing.

With a steady breath, I closed my eyes and whispered once more, "Thank you, God." Thank you for the unexpected moments, the surprising growth, and the people who come into our lives when we least expect it. I didn't know what the future held."

 I was certain of one thing: whatever happened next, Sutton and I would face it together. The letter meant more to me than I could express.

As I sat there, holding the paper in my hands, I felt a deep sense of gratitude wash over me. It wasn't just the words that had touched me, it was the courage behind them. Sutton had taken the time to write everything out, to share parts of himself that had always been hidden. It was a gift, a glimpse into his heart, and I knew I would treasure it forever. This wasn't just about a thank-you; it was a doorway, an invitation to something deeper. And I was ready to walk through it. I ran my fingers over the edges of the paper, carefully folding it back and placing it in the drawer of my desk, where I kept the things I wanted to keep safe.

But Sutton's letter wasn't something I could just file away. No, it deserved more than that. It deserved a place where I could revisit it, where I could be reminded of the honesty and vulnerability he had shown me. I had always been the kind of person to hold onto moments that mattered, to keep the things that touched my heart in plain sight. This letter would be one of those things.

As I sat back in my chair, my mind wandered. I thought about how much this letter meant to me, how much it meant to *us*. It wasn't just the words themselves, it was what they represented: the journey we had been on together, the quiet moments of support, the unspoken connection that had been growing between us. Every word in Sutton's letter felt like a promise, a glimpse of the future we could build together, if we were brave enough to face it. I couldn't stop thinking about how far Sutton had come. When I first met him, he had been guarded, closed off, even a little cynical. But now, here he was, opening up in a way I had never imagined. It was as if the walls he had built around himself had started to crumble, and in their place, something new was emerging. It was hard to imagine just how much courage that had taken, especially given everything he had been through with Maggie, with the pain and the heartbreak.

On my way home that night, still clutching the letter in my hand, I stopped at a small shop near campus. The warm lights of the store beckoned me inside, and I found myself drawn to the aisles filled with all kinds of supplies. I wasn't sure why I was there, but something inside me told me I needed to do this. I walked to the corner where they kept the boxes and found a simple, wooden one that spoke to me. It was plain, unassuming, but it had potential, much like Sutton had been when I first met him. I picked it up and took it to the counter, feeling a sense of purpose with every step. I bought the box and brought it back to my dorm room, where I spent the next hour decorating it. I covered it with soft, calming colors, with patterns that made me think of quiet, peaceful moments.

As I worked, I carefully cut out small pieces of paper with snippets from Sutton's letter, words that had stayed with me since I read them. I glued them to the box, each one carefully placed, each one a reminder of the journey we had begun together. When I finished, I sat back and looked at the box. It was simple, but it felt like a piece of art, a representation of all the things that had shaped us, the moments we had shared, and the hope I had for the future.

On the top, I wrote a single word: *"Growing."*

It felt fitting, for that was what we were both doing. In our own ways, we were learning, changing, and becoming more than we had been before. I placed the letter inside the box, along with the other small mementos I had kept from my journey with Sutton. And as I closed the lid, I realized something. This wasn't just a box to hold memories, it was a symbol of what we had built together so far, and what we would continue to build in the days ahead.

As I looked down at the box in my lap, a smile spread across my face, wide and genuine. For the first time in a long time, I felt a sense of peace and happiness fill me from the inside out, my heart light and free. I couldn't help but smile ear to ear, feeling like I was finally on the right path, happier than I had ever been.

17

As the new spring semester began, I found myself standing at the threshold of a new chapter, one filled with challenges, opportunities, and the constant reminder of why I had chosen this path.

My days were now filled with lectures, labs, and hands-on training in subjects that both excited and overwhelmed me. Anatomy, Nurse Aid, and CNA courses demanded every ounce of focus I could muster, but they also filled me with a deep sense of purpose.

Walking into my anatomy class on the first day, I was struck by the sheer complexity of what we were about to study. The professor introduced the syllabus with a seriousness that made me sit up straighter in my chair. The human body, a masterpiece of creation, was now my textbook, my puzzle to unravel.

As I flipped through the pages of the dense textbook, I couldn't help but marvel at the intricacies of God's design. Every system, every organ, every cell seemed to speak of His divine handiwork. I whispered a quiet prayer of thanks, asking for the strength and clarity to navigate this demanding course. The first lab session was both exhilarating and intimidating. We were tasked with identifying various bones in the skeletal system. Standing over the plastic skeleton laid out before me, I felt a mix of awe and determination. I ran my fingers over the smooth, cool surface of the femur and thought about how much it represented, strength, balance, mobility. These weren't just bones; they were the framework of life.

While working through the lab, jotting notes and memorizing terms, I silently prayed for focus and retention. Anatomy wasn't just about memorization, though. It was about understanding how everything connected, how the body worked as one cohesive unit. The heart's rhythm, the lungs' expansion, the muscles' contraction, all of it reminded me of how God had crafted us with such care. Even when the material grew dense and overwhelming, I felt a sense of peace knowing that this was part of a larger plan. Each late-night study session and every quiz was a step toward the calling God had placed on my heart. Nurse Aide training was a completely different experience.

This course was less about theory and more about application. We learned how to care for patients with dignity and compassion. The skills we practiced, taking vital signs, transferring patients, assisting with daily activities, weren't just technical tasks. They were acts of service, opportunities to reflect God's love in small but meaningful ways.

Our instructor often reminded us that being a nurse aide wasn't just about skill; it was about heart.

"You're walking into someone's most vulnerable moments," she said one day.

"How you treat them matters. It's not just what you do but how you do it."

Her words stayed with me, resonating deeply. I thought about the countless people I would encounter in this line of work, each with their own stories, struggles, and hopes. I prayed that I would always have the grace to see them as God does, worthy, valued, and loved. The CNA course built upon what I was learning in Nurse Aide training. It was more rigorous, with clinical rotations that brought us face-to-face with real patients in real settings. My first day at the clinical site was nerve-wracking.

As I walked into the long-term care facility, the smell of antiseptic mixed with the faint scent of lavender air freshener greeted me. The sounds of beeping monitors and soft conversations filled the air. My heart raced as I introduced myself to the staff and residents. One of my first tasks was assisting an elderly woman named Mrs. Dawson with her breakfast.

Her hands trembled slightly as she reached for the spoon, and I gently guided her, offering a warm smile.

"Thank you, dear," she said, her voice frail but kind.

That moment reaffirmed why I was here. It wasn't just about completing tasks; it was about making a difference, however small.

Later that day, as I helped a patient transition from their wheelchair to their bed, I felt a surge of gratitude for the strength and skills God had given me. This work was hard, both physically and emotionally, but it was also deeply fulfilling. Every interaction was an opportunity to serve, to show kindness, to be the hands and feet of Christ. Back in the classroom, we delved deeper into the technical aspects of care. We learned about infection control, medical terminology, and patient rights. Each topic added another layer to my understanding of what it meant to care for others. Our instructor often emphasized the importance of integrity in this field.

"Patients trust you with their lives," she said. "That trust is sacred. Don't take it lightly."

Her words struck a chord with me. I prayed that I would always honor that trust, no matter how challenging the work became. There were days when the workload felt overwhelming, when the long hours of studying and clinicals left me drained. But even in those moments, I felt God's presence. I would pause, take a deep breath, and remind myself that I wasn't doing this alone. God had called me to this path, and He would equip me to walk it.

Philippians 4:13 became my mantra: *"I can do all things through Christ who strengthens me."*

On particularly tough days, I found solace in small acts of gratitude. I would take a moment to thank God for the opportunity to learn, for the professors who challenged me, and for the classmates who journeyed alongside me. I even started keeping a journal where I wrote down moments of joy and growth, a resident's smile, a successful lab session, a kind word from a peer. These small victories reminded me that progress, no matter how incremental, was still progress. One afternoon, as I sat in the library reviewing my anatomy notes, I felt a wave of clarity. The complexity of the material no longer felt intimidating but inspiring. The human body wasn't just a subject to study; it was a testament to God's brilliance. Every system, every process, every detail pointed to a Creator who cared deeply about His creation. I whispered a prayer of thanks, marveling at the privilege of studying something so profound.

As the days passed and weeks went on, I noticed how much my perspective was shifting. I was no longer just a student trying to pass exams; I was someone preparing to make a difference. My classes weren't just about gaining knowledge; they were about equipping myself to serve others with compassion and excellence.

Every lecture, every lab, every clinical rotation was a step closer to fulfilling God's purpose for my life. One evening, as I walked back to my dorm after a long day of classes and clinicals, I stopped at the chapel on campus.

The quiet stillness of the space invited me in, and I knelt at one of the pews.

"Thank You, Lord," I whispered. "Thank You for guiding me, for giving me the strength to keep going. I know this journey isn't easy, but I trust that You're with me every step of the way."

In that moment, I felt a deep sense of peace. The challenges ahead didn't feel as daunting, and the uncertainties of the future didn't weigh as heavily. I left the chapel with a renewed sense of purpose, ready to face whatever came next. My classes continued to challenge and shape me, pushing me to grow not just academically but spiritually and emotionally. I began to see how every lesson, every experience, was preparing me for the work God had called me to do. And for that, I was endlessly grateful. In the quiet moments of reflection, my thoughts often drifted to Sutton. As I immersed myself in my studies, I couldn't help but think about how much he had grown over the past few months. Sutton had faced challenges of his own, yet he'd emerged stronger, more compassionate, and more grounded in his faith. I found myself marveling at how much he'd changed, not just for himself but for those around him. His journey inspired me to keep going, even when the path ahead seemed uncertain. Sutton had become a source of encouragement for me in ways I hadn't anticipated. His unwavering support during my most stressful moments reminded me of the power of friendship and the beauty of having someone who truly believes in you.

He'd taught me to find joy in the small victories and to trust in God's timing, even when life felt overwhelming. In turn, I hoped that I had been a positive influence in his life as well. I prayed that my words and actions had shown him the love and grace of Christ, just as he had done for me. There were times when I'd catch myself smiling, thinking about how Sutton's kindness had brought so much light into my days. His transformation wasn't just about him; it was a testament to God's ability to work in and through us.

Watching him grow had strengthened my own faith, reminding me that change was possible, even in the most difficult circumstances. One evening, after a particularly long day of classes, I found myself scrolling through my phone, looking at old messages from Sutton. His words of encouragement, his genuine care, they meant more to me than I could put into words.

The semester continued, Sutton's impact on my life became even more evident. He had a way of lighting up even the darkest days with his humor and kind-hearted nature. There were moments when I would feel overwhelmed by the weight of my responsibilities, but just a simple message from Sutton would remind me that I wasn't alone. It was as if God had placed him in my life at just the right moment, a reminder that we don't have to walk our journeys alone. His friendship was more than just a comfort, it was a constant source of encouragement, pushing me to keep moving forward. Sutton and I had grown so much since those early days of misunderstanding and friction. Looking back, I realized how important those struggles had been for our growth. We had faced challenges together, and while they hadn't always been easy, they had strengthened our bond. Through every disagreement, every moment of doubt, we had found ways to reconcile and move forward, learning not only about each other but about ourselves. It was in those moments of conflict that we were given the chance to become better versions of ourselves.

One evening, as we sat together after class in the dorm's common area, Sutton and I talked about the future. The excitement of our impending graduation filled the air as we shared our dreams and aspirations. Sutton talked about his desire to become a doctor, and I shared my passion for becoming a NICU nurse. It was clear that we both had a calling that we were eager to pursue, but what struck me most was how much our faith had guided us to these paths. In every conversation, every plan we made for the future, God's presence was evident, and I was reminded of how He had orchestrated every step of our journey. Sutton's growth wasn't just in his academics or career aspirations; it was in his character. I had witnessed firsthand how his faith had transformed him, how he had become more patient, compassionate, and understanding. I saw it in the way he interacted with others, how he would go out of his way to lend a hand or offer a kind word. It was no longer just about his goals or ambitions, it was about how he could serve others. His example served as a reminder to me that our faith isn't just something we hold privately but something that should be reflected in the way we live our lives.

There were times when I would see Sutton's quiet acts of service and realize that, in many ways, we were both living out our faith in the work we were doing.

Sutton's passion for helping others through medicine and my desire to care for those in need through nursing were both expressions of God's love in action. We had found our purpose, and it was in serving others. In those quiet moments of reflection, I couldn't help but feel a deep sense of gratitude for the journey we had taken together. Our friendship had become a testament to how God's plans for our lives unfold in ways we could never predict but always recognize in hindsight.

The end of the semester drew near, I found myself filled with a sense of peace and anticipation. The challenges of college, the struggles of balancing faith with academics, had all been part of the preparation for the lives we were about to step into. Sutton and I, having walked through these years together, were now poised to take on the next chapter of our lives. I prayed that we would continue to grow, to support each other, and to follow God's calling with unwavering trust. As I looked at Sutton and thought about everything we had been through, I couldn't help but feel incredibly thankful for the journey, for the lessons, and most of all, for the friendship that had been such a powerful part of it all. I thought about how far we'd come, and how much farther we will go. Sutton Adams has made my college year a roller coaster.

From the chaotic blaming, and unnecessary amount of arguments, we have came so far.

18

Early days of the semester had set the pace, a whirlwind of lectures, labs, and clinicals that left little room for anything else.

By the time I reached February, the rhythm of it all began to feel slightly more manageable. I'd found a balance between academics, work, and the friendships that kept me grounded. Yet, in the stillness of certain evenings, when the world felt quieter, I realized there were deeper lessons waiting to be uncovered. One such evening, after a long day of CNA clinicals, I returned to my dorm room to find Kelli sprawled across her bed, a football magazine in hand. Her face lit up when she saw me.

"You look exhausted," she teased, tossing the magazine onto her nightstand. I dropped my bag onto the floor and collapsed onto my bed.

"That's because I am. Today was... a lot."

"Tell me about it." Kelli sat up, tucking her legs beneath her.

Despite her usual bubbly demeanor, there was a calmness to her tonight that invited me to share. I recounted my day, the delicate balance of learning to care for patients while also managing the emotional weight of it all. I told her about Mr. Alvarez, a patient who'd shared stories of his younger years in the military, and Mrs. Dawson, whose health was declining despite our best efforts.

"It's hard," I admitted, my voice quieter. "To see people in pain and know that there's only so much you can do. But at the same time, it's a privilege to be there for them, even in small ways."

Kelli nodded thoughtfully. "You're doing something that matters, Claire. Don't forget that."

Her words were simple, but they carried weight. As we talked, I realized how much Kelli had become my anchor in this season of life. She didn't just listen, she understood. Later that night, after Kelli had fallen asleep, I pulled out my journal. The habit of writing had become a refuge for me, a way to process the highs and lows of each day.

As I scribbled down my thoughts, I found myself reflecting on something our CNA instructor had said earlier that week: "Compassion doesn't mean you have to fix everything. It means being present, even when things are hard."

Those words stayed with me, challenging the perfectionist in me that always wanted to do more, be more. I thought about Mrs. Dawson, how I'd sat with her for a few moments after helping her back to bed. She hadn't said much, but the way her eyes softened and her lips curved into a faint smile told me that my presence had mattered. Sometimes, it wasn't about the big gestures or solving every problem. Sometimes, it was about simply showing up. The following week, I found myself leaning into the quiet moments more intentionally.

One morning before class, I stopped by the chapel again. The stillness there was becoming a sanctuary, a space where I could pause and realign my heart.

"Lord," I whispered, sitting in one of the pews, "thank You for the strength to keep going. Thank You for the people You've placed in my life, my patients, my classmates, Kelli, and Sutton. Help me to see each moment as an opportunity to serve You."

 The prayer wasn't long or eloquent, but it came from a place of honesty. As I left the chapel, I felt a renewed sense of peace, as if God was reminding me that I didn't have to carry the weight of everything alone. My friendship with Sutton had grown deeper in ways I hadn't expected. He'd become a constant source of encouragement, always seeming to know when I needed a kind word or a simple reminder to breathe. Thursday evening, he called just as I was about to start a marathon study session.

"Hey," his voice was warm, grounding me instantly. "How's my favorite future nurse doing?"

I laughed, the stress of the day easing a bit.

"Tired. Overwhelmed. But I'm hanging in there."

"Good. You're stronger than you think, you know that?"

"Some days I'm not so sure," I admitted.

"Well, I am," he said firmly. "And I'm pretty sure God is too."

His words made me pause. Sutton's own journey of faith had been transformative, and seeing him lean into it so fully was both inspiring and humbling. We talked for a while longer, about everything and nothing.

By the time we parted, I felt lighter, as if the burdens of the day had been shared.

I noticed how much these quiet moments, whether in the chapel, in conversations with Kelli and Sutton, or in the stillness of my own reflections, were shaping me. They reminded me that growth didn't always happen in the chaos of busy days.

Sometimes, it was in the pauses, the moments of stillness, that God did His most profound work. One afternoon, during a rare break between classes, I found myself sitting on a bench outside the library. The sun was warm on my face, and the sounds of campus life buzzed around me. For the first time in weeks, I wasn't rushing to the next thing. I opened my anatomy textbook, intending to review a few chapters, but my eyes kept drifting to the world around me, the rustle of leaves in the breeze, the laughter of students passing by, the intricate patterns of sunlight filtering through the trees. It struck me, in that moment, how much beauty there was in simply being present.

I closed the textbook and leaned back, letting the stillness wash over me.

"Thank You, Lord," I whispered. "For this moment, for this season, for everything You're teaching me."

In that quiet space, I felt a clarity and peace that no amount of studying could provide. I didn't have all the answers, and I certainly didn't have everything figured out. But I knew I was exactly where I was supposed to be, and that was enough.

That night, Kelli suggested something unexpected. "Let's go to the next football game. You've been buried in your textbooks for weeks, and I think you need a break."

Her enthusiasm was contagious, and for the first time, I didn't feel the need to resist.

"You know what? Let's do it."

The game was *ELECTRIC*. Hearing the roar of the crowd, the crisp night air, and the joy of being surrounded by people who shared the same passion.

Kelli's laughter rang out beside me, and I realized how much I'd missed moments like this. Sutton had texted earlier to say he'd be there too, and as I glanced across the stands, I spotted him, his hand raised in a wave. In that moment, surrounded by friends and the vibrancy of campus life, I felt a deep sense of gratitude. God had placed me here, in this season, with these people for a reason. And while the challenges were many, the blessings were even greater.

"This is what it's all about," I thought to myself. "Finding joy in the journey, even when it's hard."

As the game ended and we made our way back to the dorms, Kelli threw her arm around my shoulder.

"See? You needed this."

She was right. I needed the reminder that life wasn't just about striving, it was also about savoring the moments that made it all worthwhile. Thank you Jesus. As the semester continued, Sutton's impact on my life became even more evident. He had a way of lighting up even the darkest days with his humor and kind-hearted nature. There were moments when I would feel overwhelmed by the weight of my responsibilities, but just a simple message from Sutton would remind me that I wasn't alone. It was as if God had placed him in my life at just the right moment, a reminder that we don't have to walk our journeys alone. His friendship was more than just a comfort, it was a constant source of encouragement, pushing me to keep moving forward.

Sutton and I had grown so much since those early days of misunderstanding and friction. Looking back, I realized how important those struggles had been for our growth. We had faced challenges together, and while they hadn't always been easy, they had strengthened our bond.

Through every disagreement, every moment of doubt, we had found ways to reconcile and move forward, learning not only about each other but about ourselves. It was in those moments of conflict that we were given the chance to become better versions of ourselves. One evening, as we sat together after class in the dorm's common area, Sutton and I talked about the future. The excitement of our impending graduation filled the air as we shared our dreams and aspirations. Sutton talked about his desire to become a doctor, and I shared my passion for becoming a NICU nurse.

It was clear that we both had a calling that we were eager to pursue, but what struck me most was how much our faith had guided us to these paths. In every conversation, every plan we made for the future, God's presence was evident, and I was reminded of how He had orchestrated every step of our journey. Sutton's growth wasn't just in his academics or career aspirations; it was in his character. I had witnessed firsthand how his faith had transformed him, how he had become more patient, compassionate, and understanding. I saw it in the way he interacted with others, how he would go out of his way to lend a hand or offer a kind word. It was no longer just about his goals or ambitions, it was about how he could serve others. His example served as a reminder to me that our faith isn't just something we hold privately but something that should be reflected in the way we live our lives. There were times when I would see Sutton's quiet acts of service and realize that, in many ways, we were both living out our faith in the work we were doing. Sutton's passion for helping others through medicine and my desire to care for those in need through nursing were both expressions of God's love in action. We had found our purpose, and it was in serving others. In those quiet moments of reflection, I couldn't help but feel a deep sense of gratitude for the journey we had taken together. Our friendship had become a testament to how God's plans for our lives unfold in ways we could never predict but always recognize in hindsight. As the end of the semester drew near, I found myself filled with a sense of peace and anticipation. The challenges of college, the struggles of balancing faith with academics, had all been part of the preparation for the lives we were about to step into. Sutton and I, having walked through these years together, were now poised to take on the next chapter of our lives. I prayed that we would continue to grow, to support each other, and to follow God's calling with unwavering trust. As I looked at Sutton and thought about everything we had been through, I couldn't help but feel incredibly thankful for the journey, for the lessons, and most of all, for the friendship that had been such a powerful part of it all. Can not thank my God enough.

19

Wow.

The following weeks felt like they were moving in an uncountable fast forward in time. The rhythm of school, clinicals, and friendships had found a steady pace, but beneath it all, something had shifted. Something that felt bigger than the coursework or even the days spent in the clinic. Sutton had become more than just a friend, he was someone I could lean on in ways that were difficult to explain. There was an ease in our conversations, a connection that seemed to grow stronger with each passing day.

Even the quiet moments shared over the phone or during brief campus encounters felt significant, as if each one was a piece of a much larger story unfolding. One evening, after a particularly exhausting day of studying, Sutton called to check in. We spoke about everything and nothing, the mundane details of our day, the professors who had made us roll our eyes, the funny things Kelli had said earlier. But beneath the surface, there was a deeper current, one that had been quietly building between us.

"You know, I'm really glad we've gotten closer this semester," Sutton said, his voice warm and genuine.

"It's been a crazy few months, but I feel like we're both in a place where we really get each other."

I smiled, feeling the weight of his words.

"I'm glad too, Sutton. You've become someone I really trust. I'm not sure what I'd do without you."

It wasn't the first time we'd said something like that to each other, but this time, the sincerity in his voice resonated deeper within me. Sutton wasn't just a constant source of encouragement anymore; he was becoming someone who had a special place in my heart. I couldn't deny it, there was something more here, something that felt right. The weekend came, and with it, the much-anticipated football game. Kelli had been excited about it for weeks, urging me to come along despite the workload that seemed never-ending. I had agreed, finally giving myself permission to take a break. The stadium was electric with energy as the crowd buzzed in anticipation. Sutton's team was on the brink of victory, and I could feel the tension in the air. Sutton was playing quarterback, and the stakes were high. It was the fourth quarter, and his team was down by just a few points. With only seconds left on the clock, it was clear that this would be the moment to either win or lose the game.

My heart raced as I watched him stand behind the line, his eyes focused and determined. I had seen him practice countless times, but nothing compared to the intensity of this moment.

As the ball was snapped, Sutton dropped back, scanning the field with precision. The stadium erupted into a roar as he launched the ball into the air, a perfect spiral spiraling toward the end zone. Time seemed to stand still as the receiver leaped into the air, catching the ball just before the defenders could intercept. Touchdown.

The crowd went wild, and my heart swelled with pride for him. Sutton had done it, he had just thrown the game-winning touchdown. But what happened next took my breath away. With the game officially secured, Sutton didn't celebrate with his teammates. Instead, he ran straight toward the stands, his eyes locked on mine. My heart skipped a beat as he reached the sideline, and before I knew it, he was climbing up the stairs of the stadium toward me.

He reached the top, his hands finding mine as the crowd cheered around us.

Without a word, Sutton leaned in and *kissed me*.

The kiss was nothing like I had ever expected.

It was raw, full of emotion, every ounce of relief, joy, and love that had been building between us since the first moment we'd truly connected.

I was so stunned that for a moment, I forgot to breathe.

The world seemed to blur around us, and all that mattered was him, standing there, holding me. Before I could fully process what was happening, Sutton stepped back slightly and smiled. The joy in his eyes was unmistakable, and I felt a rush of emotions, surprise, disbelief, happiness, and something deeper, something that told me this was the beginning of something truly meaningful.

Without thinking, I jumped off the stands, my arms reaching for him. Sutton caught me easily, lifting me into his embrace, and I buried my face against his chest, overwhelmed by the flood of emotions coursing through me.

"I didn't expect that," I whispered, still trying to catch my breath.

Sutton grinned, his voice soft but confident. "Neither did I, but I couldn't let that moment pass without showing you how much you mean to me." My heart fluttered as I gazed up at him, realizing just how much this moment, this kiss, this connection, meant to me.

In a world that had felt so chaotic and uncertain at times, Sutton had become my anchor. And now, with the weight of everything we had shared between us, I knew that we had something real.

As we stood there, wrapped in each other's arms, I realized that sometimes, the most beautiful moments are the ones that catch you off guard. And in that moment, amidst the roar of the crowd and the excitement of the game, I knew that God had placed Sutton in my life for a reason. And whatever came next, we would face it together. As the night wore on and the excitement of the game slowly faded into the quiet hum of the campus, I found myself walking back with Sutton, our hands still entwined. The world around us seemed distant, muffled by the overwhelming sense of peace that lingered after the whirlwind of the game and the kiss.

My mind replayed the events over and over, and as we walked side by side, I couldn't help but let my thoughts wander. I found myself thinking back to all the moments we had shared over the past months, the late-night conversations, the laughter, the comfort of his presence when I felt overwhelmed. It had all felt so natural, so right. There was a certain rhythm to us, an ease that made it feel as though we had always been meant to find each other. But as I walked, something stirred inside of me, a question that had been quietly forming in my mind over the past few days, ever since the kiss and everything that had unfolded between us. I paused for a moment, just a step behind Sutton, and the question rose to the surface, clear and unspoken:

Is this the path You wanted us to have, Lord?

The question was not one of doubt, but of surrender. Was this relationship part of the plan You had designed for me, for him? Did You bring us together for a reason that I had yet to fully understand? I couldn't help but feel a deep sense of gratitude for how Sutton had become such a pivotal part of my life, but also a humble awareness that everything was in His hands. No matter how perfect it seemed, I needed to trust that the steps we were taking, together or apart, were in His care. I caught up to Sutton, smiling softly as I walked beside him. The uncertainty in my heart faded just a

little, knowing that no matter what the future held, I
didn't have to navigate it alone. As the weeks passed, I
began to realize just how much those moments of
stillness and connection mattered. Life at college could
be a whirlwind, full of assignments, clinical hours, and
the constant pull of expectations. But I had learned that
it wasn't in the hustle that I found peace, it was in the
pauses, in the times when I allowed myself to simply
breathe, to look around and appreciate the small
blessings.

Each moment, whether it was a conversation with
Kelli, a text from Sutton, or a quiet prayer in the
chapel, became a reminder that God was always near,
working in ways I couldn't always see but could
always trust. The next few weeks seemed to fly by in a
blur of tests, clinical shifts, and group projects. But
even amidst the busyness, I held onto the lessons I had
learned in the stillness.

When things felt overwhelming, I found solace in
simple moments of connection. Whether it was taking
a few minutes to call Sutton just to hear his voice or
sitting quietly with Kelli as we reviewed our notes
together, I knew I wasn't alone. God had placed people
in my life who supported me, prayed for me, and
reminded me of the beauty of walking alongside
others. In these relationships, I saw His love and
provision.

As I stood there, wrapped in Sutton's arms, the world
seemed to fade into the background, leaving just the
two of us. The heat of the moment still lingered

between us, the adrenaline from the game mixing with the warmth of his touch.

"You know," I said, my voice teasing as I looked up at him with a grin, "I think you've just set the bar for first kiss pretty high."

Sutton laughed softly, his hand gently brushing the hair away from my face. "Well, I had to make it memorable. Don't want to disappoint after a game-winning moment, right?"

His eyes sparkled with mischief, and I felt my heart flutter. It was the kind of moment I had always dreamed of, something so simple yet so significant.

"I think you're officially my favorite quarterback," I teased, unable to keep the smile off my face.

His grin widened, his hand still holding mine with a reassuring squeeze. I rolled my eyes playfully, nudging him gently. The spark in his eyes told me he loved this back-and-forth, the banter that was slowly growing into something more. As we walked hand in hand through the stadium, I couldn't help but smile to myself. The night had turned into something I'd never forget, and I was more than ready for whatever came next between us.

A random evening, as I was preparing for another clinical rotation, I received an unexpected message from Mrs. Dawson's daughter.

"I just wanted to thank you for everything you've done for my mom. She always speaks so highly of you, and it means the world to us," the message read.

I paused, reading it over again. Mrs. Dawson had become one of those patients whose memory I would carry with me, not because of the medical procedures I had helped with, but because of the quiet moments I had spent with her. It was a reminder that sometimes, the most meaningful acts of service don't involve grand gestures, they're in the small moments of care, the unspoken compassion that makes a person feel seen and valued. That night, I found myself reflecting on how God had called me into this field of nursing, not just to treat the body, but to care for the soul. I had come to understand that healing wasn't just about fixing physical ailments, it was about offering peace in times of pain, offering hope when it felt distant, and providing comfort when nothing else seemed certain. I had been given the incredible privilege of walking alongside people during some of their most vulnerable moments, and I knew this was exactly where I was meant to be.

My faith, my journey, and my purpose all seemed to converge in these quiet moments of service. I continued to find strength in the little things, like the smile of a patient after a difficult procedure or the kind words of a professor who recognized my hard work. But I also realized that God was teaching me lessons outside the classroom. He was teaching me about patience, about humility, about trusting in His timing. Sometimes the answers didn't come right away, and sometimes the results weren't as immediate as I had hoped. But I was learning that faith wasn't just about seeing immediate results, it was about trusting that God was at work, even when the outcome was still unfolding. One Sunday evening, after spending the afternoon studying, I sat outside in the quiet of the campus courtyard. The sky was painted with hues of pink and orange as the sun began to set. I felt a deep sense of gratitude wash over me as I looked around at the world, the beauty of creation, the people in my life, the journey I was on. I closed my eyes and whispered a prayer of thanksgiving.

"Lord, thank You for this season of learning, for the opportunity to serve, and for the reminder that You are with me every step of the way. Help me to stay present, to stay faithful, and to continue walking the path You've set before me."

The semester continued to unfold, and as I approached the final weeks of my CNA course, I began to reflect on how much I had grown. Not just in terms of knowledge or skills, but in heart. I had learned to embrace the challenges, to see them as opportunities to grow in faith and character. As I sat in the chapel one final time before the end of the semester, I prayed a prayer of surrender, trusting that everything I had learned and experienced was part of God's greater plan for my life. I was ready for whatever came next, knowing that with God's presence and the support of those around me, I could face any challenge with strength, grace, and hope. The following days felt surreal, as if everything that had led up to the kiss had suddenly fallen into place. There was an undeniable shift in my heart, but also an underlying sense of peace that reminded me of the deeper purpose behind all of it.

As much as I had been swept up in the excitement of the game, the kiss, and the connection that had grown between Sutton and me, I knew that I needed to keep my focus on the bigger picture. I had worked hard to find balance in my life, between school, work, and friendships, and I didn't want to lose sight of that now, especially when something so significant had happened. Sutton had become a significant part of my life, but I also knew that my path was about more than just our relationship. It was about pursuing my calling, my purpose, and living in a way that honored my faith.

That week, I found myself reflecting on everything that had brought me to this point. I remembered the early days of nursing school, when I felt uncertain, unsure of how I would balance it all. I thought about the people who had helped me grow: Kelli, with her unwavering support; Sutton, whose presence had given me courage when I needed it most; and my patients, whose stories of strength and resilience continued to inspire me. I couldn't help but smile at the thought of all the relationships and moments that had shaped me. It was clear that every step of this journey had purpose. Each conversation, each challenge, and each blessing had been woven together by God's hand, guiding me toward something bigger than I could comprehend.

And while I didn't know what the future held, I had learned to trust in the process, knowing that He was in control. I knew that Sutton and I had to take things one step at a time. While the kiss had opened up a new chapter for us, it also came with new questions. What did this relationship look like now? How would it evolve? We hadn't talked much about the future yet, but I knew that the foundation we had built over the last few months, rooted in friendship, respect, and shared values, was strong.

Still, there was a part of me that needed to remain patient and prayerful. I didn't want to rush anything, but rather allow things to unfold in their own time. I trusted that God had brought Sutton into my life for a reason, and I wanted to honor that by making sure I stayed grounded in my faith and values as our relationship continued to grow.

One evening, as I sat in the chapel alone, I felt a deep sense of gratitude wash over me. It was a quiet moment, just me and God. The world outside seemed distant, and the weight of the semester seemed lighter for a brief moment. I prayed silently, thanking God for all that had come together in my life, my friends, my studies, my calling to nursing, and most of all, for Sutton. I asked for guidance and clarity, for wisdom in the steps ahead.

"Lord, I know I can't control everything, but I trust that You've got it all in Your hands. Help me to trust You in the process, and to honor the relationships You've placed in my life."

I left the chapel that night feeling renewed and at peace, knowing that no matter what came next, I wasn't walking this journey alone.

As the weeks went by, Sutton and I continued to grow closer. We shared more moments together, quiet walks across campus, deep conversations, and laughter. There was a certain ease in our relationship now, a sense of comfort that came from knowing we could be real with each other. Our time together felt like a gift, but we also made sure to give each other the space we needed to continue pursuing our individual goals. Sutton was still focused on his path toward becoming a doctor, and I was determined to stay true to my own calling as a nurse. We supported each other, but we also knew that we couldn't lose sight of our personal journeys.

What made our relationship so special was the balance we had found: two individuals walking side by side, but always with the understanding that we were both still in the process of becoming who God had designed us to be.cOne afternoon, as we sat together in the campus café, I realized that the love I had for Sutton wasn't just about the romantic moments or the excitement of being together. It was about the deeper connection we shared, the way he encouraged me, the way we prayed for each other, and the way we respected each other's dreams and aspirations. I had always believed that relationships built on mutual respect, shared faith, and a commitment to growth were the strongest kind.

And as I looked at Sutton, I knew that what we had was something real, something rooted in a foundation that could withstand the challenges ahead. I didn't know what the future held, but I knew that with him by my side, I was ready to face whatever came next.

And in that moment, I felt an overwhelming sense of peace, knowing that God was guiding us both, step by step, toward the plans He had for us.

20

The following week after the football game passed in a haze of joy and contemplation.

Sutton and I, still basking in the glow of that night, found ourselves closer than ever. Our connection had deepened in ways that felt both natural and profound, but beneath the excitement, I couldn't shake the question that had lingered in my heart:

Is this the path You wanted us to have, Lord?

I didn't have answers right away, and maybe I wasn't meant to. But as I spent more time with Sutton, laughing with him, studying together, sharing those quiet moments that seemed to say everything, I realized something. Whether or not I had the clarity I was seeking, what mattered most was that I was trusting Him with every step. And in that trust, I was finding peace.

One afternoon, as I sat in the library, the warm sunlight streaming through the windows, I thought about how far I had come since the beginning of the semester. My life had been a blur of lectures, clinicals, and friendships, but somewhere in the midst of it all, I had found a rhythm. I had found balance, not just in my studies and work, but in my relationships. And of course, in my growing connection with Sutton. That evening, after a long study session, I met Sutton outside the library. He was leaning against a tree, as casual and easy as always, but there was something different in the way he smiled at me.

 A kind of knowing, like he could sense the question that had been quietly echoing in my mind.

"How's the studying going?" he asked, pushing himself off the tree and falling into step beside me.

"It's going," I said with a half-laugh, the weight of the books in my bag suddenly feeling heavier. "I think I need a break."

Sutton nodded knowingly. "Good call. How about we grab dinner? I know a spot off-campus that serves the best burgers."

 I smiled, appreciating how he always seemed to know what I needed. As we walked toward the exit of campus, I found myself thinking about all the times he had been my support, encouraging me when I felt like I couldn't go on, reminding me of my strength when I doubted it. It wasn't just the big moments that stood out, but the little ones too: the quiet conversations in the dorm, the texts that seemed to come at exactly the right time, the way he made me laugh when I needed it most.

As we sat at the small diner, our conversation flowed easily, but there was an underlying current of something deeper between us. I couldn't quite put it into words, but it was there, unspoken, in the way we glanced at each other or shared a knowing smile.

I thought back to the question I had asked myself earlier that day, whether this relationship, this path, was part of God's plan.

Was it? Did God have something bigger in mind for us than we could see right now?

I didn't have the answer, but what I did know was that I was right where I needed to be. And with Sutton by my side, I felt more confident in the journey ahead. After dinner, we walked back to campus in the cool evening air, the conversation still flowing easily between us.

When we reached my dorm, Sutton stopped and turned to face me. His eyes were serious now, and I could tell he had something on his mind.

"Claire," he began, his voice quiet but steady, "I've been thinking a lot about us... about everything. I know we're both navigating this season of life, with all its ups and downs. But I want you to know that I'm here for you. No matter what."

The sincerity in his words touched something deep inside of me. For all the uncertainty I had felt in the past, Sutton's words gave me a sense of peace. The future was unknown, but I knew we would face it together, trusting God every step of the way.

"I know," I said softly, my heart full. "I'm here for you too."

He smiled then, and for a moment, everything felt exactly as it should. We didn't have all the answers, but we had each other. And with that, I felt ready to keep walking forward, one step at a time.

I headed up the stairs to my dorm room, I glanced back at Sutton, standing there in the soft glow of the streetlamp. There was still so much ahead, but as I stood there, I knew that whatever came next, we would be ready for it, together.

As my senior year at UNC was ending, it was a whirlwind. It felt as if time had suddenly sped up, the days slipping through my fingers like sand. The pressure of final exams, clinical rotations, and looming job applications had me constantly on edge. There were moments when I felt like I couldn't breathe, the weight of everything pulling me in so many directions. I had always been someone who tried to plan for the future, but now that it was here, the uncertainty of what came next felt overwhelming.

I had made up my mind, after months of reflection and research, I knew I wanted to become a NICU nurse. The tiny lives, the delicate care they needed, and the hope that came with each small victory in those early moments had drawn me in like nothing else. But even though I had found my calling, the path ahead still seemed so far and filled with obstacles. I wasn't just worried about getting into a NICU unit; I was stressed about finishing school with all the demands on my time and energy. Sutton could tell I was feeling the pressure. It was in the way I barely slept, in the anxious energy that seemed to radiate from me. He'd become my steady anchor through it all, always reminding me to breathe, always reminding me that this season would pass.

One evening, after another long day of studying and classes, we sat together outside on one of the benches near the library. The campus was quiet, the stars just beginning to twinkle in the sky, and for a moment, I could feel my mind slowing down, my racing thoughts settling.

Sutton turned to me, his expression more serious than usual. "How's it going, Claire? I know you've been working yourself into the ground lately."

I let out a frustrated sigh. "It's just so much, Sutton. I'm trying to finish strong, but with everything on my plate, I don't know how I'm going to make it. The NICU is where my heart is, but I'm worried about whether I'll be ready. There's so much left to do, and I just... I don't know how I'll handle it all."

He reached over, taking my hand in his, and his touch felt grounding. "You'll handle it just like you always do. One step at a time. You've always been able to balance everything, Claire. I have no doubt you'll make it."

I smiled, though the tension in my chest didn't fully ease. "But it's not just about school. It's about this next chapter. After we graduate, what happens then? How do we start the careers we've dreamed of?"

Sutton's eyes softened, and I could see the depth of his own thoughts. "I've been thinking a lot about that too," he said. "Becoming a doctor... It's been my dream for so long, but I'm realizing that it's going to be harder than I imagined. Residency, med school, it's all so much more than I thought. But just like you, I know this is what I want to do. And we'll get there. Together."

The weight of his words hit me in that moment. Sutton and I had been in the same whirlwind, chasing our dreams, and we had both faced the pressure that came with wanting to make those dreams a reality. But there was a comfort in knowing that we weren't doing it alone. We were walking this journey side by side, even if we didn't always have the answers right now.

"We'll make it through," I said, squeezing his hand. "We just need to trust that we're on the right path, even if we can't see it clearly yet."

Sutton nodded, his smile reassuring.

"Exactly. And whatever comes next, whether it's me in med school or you in the NICU, we'll get through it. We've made it this far together, haven't we?"

I laughed softly, the tightness in my chest loosening just a little. "Yeah, we have. I think we've got this."

The night air felt lighter as we sat there, talking through our hopes and anxieties. We didn't have all the answers, and the future still felt uncertain, but in that moment, it didn't matter. We had each other, and that made all the difference.

As we stood up and walked back toward campus, the weight of the world still lingered, but so did the hope. The path ahead was still unclear, but with each step forward, I was learning to trust in the process, in God's timing, and in the fact that we were exactly where we were supposed to be. The journey was just beginning. We walked back toward campus, the hum of student life surrounding us, but for a moment, it felt like the world had slowed down, just for us. I felt the tension in my shoulders begin to ease as we strolled along the path, side by side. It was as if Sutton's presence grounded me, and everything that had felt like too much suddenly seemed more manageable.

"I keep thinking about what comes next, you know?" I said after a pause, my voice quieter this time. "Graduating, starting our careers... it's all so close now, but at the same time, it feels so far. I'm excited, but I'm scared, too."

Sutton glanced over at me, his expression soft, understanding. "I get it. I'm nervous, too. I've wanted to be a doctor my whole life, but now that it's real, it's intimidating. The work, the pressure, the long hours... it's not what I imagined back when I was just a kid dreaming about it. But I can't shake the feeling that I'm supposed to do this."

I nodded, feeling a shared weight in his words. The fear of the unknown was there for both of us, yet it was the excitement, the passion we had for our respective callings that kept us moving forward. Even though the future seemed uncertain, we both knew deep down that this was the path God had placed before us. It wasn't easy, and it wouldn't be without its challenges, but we were being shaped for something greater than we could see.

As we neared the entrance to the dorms, I looked up at Sutton.

"Do you ever wonder if we're doing the right thing? I mean, I know this is what we've wanted for so long, but... what if it's not? What if there's more to this whole thing than just getting into the career we dreamed of?"

He took a deep breath, his gaze thoughtful.

"I do wonder. A lot, actually. But maybe that's the point. Maybe the path isn't meant to be just about the destination. Maybe it's about the growth, the journey, and the people we meet along the way. That's where I think God's at work. In the process. In the steps we're taking right now, even when we don't see the whole picture."

His words settled deep in my heart. Maybe this season of life, this pressure, this uncertainty, wasn't something to be afraid of. Maybe it was the space where God was refining us, helping us become the people He created us to be. The nurses, the doctors, the individuals who would one day change lives, not just through our careers, but through the love and compassion we showed others along the way. I leaned into Sutton as we walked up the stairs to the dorm. His words had given me a renewed sense of purpose. It wasn't just about getting through school. It was about living each day with intention, with faith, trusting that every step, no matter how challenging, was part of His greater plan.

"I don't know what the future holds, Sutton," I said, my voice soft yet steady, "But I know I'm not meant to do it alone. And that makes all the difference."

Sutton squeezed my hand gently, his smile warm and reassuring. "You never will be. I'm with you, every step of the way."

As we said our goodbyes and I turned to head back to my room, I couldn't help but feel a sense of peace settle over me. I didn't have all the answers, and I didn't know exactly what the next chapter of my life would look like. But I knew one thing for sure: I was right where I needed to be. With Sutton by my side, and with God leading us forward, I was ready to face whatever came next. As the days passed, I continued to reflect on the choices that had brought me here, both the decisions I had made and the ones that had been made for me.

With every passing week, it seemed like the stakes were getting higher, and the future was drawing nearer with its heavy expectations. Graduation was no longer a distant idea, but a tangible reality that loomed in front of me. Yet, amidst the pressure, there was something freeing about finally knowing what I wanted to do.

 Becoming a NICU nurse wasn't just a career choice, it was a calling. I could already picture myself in that tiny, sterile hospital room, offering comfort to new parents, holding their fragile babies in my arms and whispering prayers over them. The thought brought me peace, but the path to get there was still uncertain and filled with challenges. I had to remember that just because I knew my destination didn't mean the journey would be without its hardships.

And that was okay.

I had to trust that everything I was experiencing, every stressful exam, every late night spent studying, as part of the process. A process that would ultimately prepare me for the work I was meant to do. Sutton, too, was facing the same sense of uncertainty, though he carried it differently. It seemed like his mind was always wrapped around the future, the medical school interviews, the residency programs, the competition. I could see how his dreams of becoming a doctor had driven him for so long, but now, the reality of it all was setting in. I admired his determination, but I also saw the weight it was placing on his shoulders. He wasn't just working hard to get into med school; he was doing it for a purpose that stretched far beyond himself. Like me, he felt called to serve, to make a difference in the lives of others. The thought of him one day saving lives, offering care to those in need, filled me with pride.

But at the same time, it made me aware of the sacrifices both of us would have to make. Long hours, missed holidays, the constant juggling of work and personal life, this was the reality of our chosen careers. But as daunting as it seemed, I knew we both shared a deep sense of purpose that would keep us grounded through it all. One evening, after a particularly grueling day of studying, I sat on the edge of my bed, staring at my textbooks spread out before me. The weight of it all felt suffocating. I had worked hard, but the looming final exams and the pressure to secure a job felt like an insurmountable mountain. It was in those moments of doubt that I had to remind myself of why I was doing this, to serve, to help, to make a difference.

I had to remember that this wasn't just about me or the next step in my career. It was about something greater. It was about living my life in a way that honored the calling God had placed on my heart. But even with that knowledge, it was hard to silence the voice in my head that questioned whether I was enough, whether I was strong enough to take on the responsibilities ahead.

What if I wasn't ready? What if I didn't make it?

These were the thoughts that circled my mind late into the night.

As I lay there, Sutton's words echoed in my mind:

"One step at a time."

They were simple, but they brought clarity. In that moment, I realized that I didn't have to have it all figured out. No one did. No one could predict the future or control what lay ahead.

But what I could do was take it one step at a time, be faithful in the little things, trust in the process, and allow myself to grow as I moved forward. I didn't have to rush the journey. Sometimes, the most important thing was simply showing up, doing the work, and trusting God to take care of the rest. It wasn't about achieving perfection or having all the answers, it was about being present, being faithful, and letting the process shape me into who I was meant to become. As the weight on my shoulders lessened just a little, I felt a sense of peace settle in my heart. And then there was Sutton, always there with his steady presence.

No matter how overwhelmed I felt or how uncertain the future seemed, he never wavered. His belief in me, in us, had been a constant source of strength. We didn't have to have it all together, and that was okay. We were a team, two individuals navigating life's challenges, supporting each other every step of the way. The thought of facing the future with him by my side filled me with a sense of purpose. We didn't know exactly what the next chapter held, but together, we would figure it out. And in the meantime, we would continue to take it one step at a time. With every shared moment, every laugh, every late-night conversation, I knew that our bond was growing stronger.

We were growing together, not just in our faith and careers, but in the trust and love that would carry us through whatever came next. And that was enough. One step at a time.

21

As always, the stadium was alive with energy, the air thick with anticipation.

Every seat was filled, every face lit with excitement as the clock ticked down. UNC had fought tooth and nail for this moment, and now, with only a few seconds left on the clock, everything was hanging in the balance. The field was a sea of motion, players sprinting, coaches shouting instructions, the band playing their fight song. It was the kind of tension you only feel in the final moments of a championship game. And then, the announcement came over the speakers: "Suspectedly this will be the last play of the game."

My heart thudded in my chest. Sutton was under center, looking calm, but I could see the fire in his eyes.

He wasn't just playing for the win, he was playing for something *deeper*.

Something that I had felt growing between us for weeks, for months, maybe even longer. But right now, it was all about the game. And as the crowd roared, I couldn't tear my eyes away from him. I had never been more proud. The ball was snapped, and Sutton's eyes scanned the field, looking for an opening.

The defense surged forward, but Sutton, calm as ever, dodged the first wave of defenders, planting his feet in the pocket.

His arm cocked back, and for a brief moment, everything seemed to freeze. And then, *WHOOSH!*

He launched the ball into the air, the spiral perfect and tight, cutting through the night sky.

The stadium fell into a breathless silence as the ball sailed toward the end zone. It seemed to hang there forever, the light from the stadium lamps reflecting off its surface. The crowd held its breath as the receiver ran full-speed toward the ball.

And then, suddenly we watched this white and tarheel blue gloves secure the ball tightly!

His hands locked onto it, and the crowd exploded. The stadium and myself were SHOOK!! The noise, the excitement, the raw energy of the fans was overwhelming.

A massive cheer echoed through the stands, reverberating off the walls and shaking the ground beneath me. People were jumping, hugging, and shouting. It was pure joy. The roar of the crowd was deafening, drowning out everything else. But even amid the chaos, my eyes were still locked on Sutton.

He was standing tall in the middle of the field, his arms raised to the sky as he looked around, a proud grin on his face. UNC had won.

The victory was ours. Sutton had done it, he had thrown the game-winning touchdown. The championship was secured, and the crowd was losing it.

The energy in the stadium was electric, and for a moment, it felt like the world had stopped. I couldn't help but scream along with everyone else, jumping up and down, celebrating like I had won something too. But as the noise of the stadium surged around me, I felt a strange sense of calm fall over me. Amid all the chaos, I knew I was waiting for something else, something bigger. I didn't know it yet, but it was about to unfold in a way that would change everything.

The loudspeaker crackled suddenly, cutting through the celebration like a sharp breath.

"Attention, everyone!" the announcer's voice boomed over the loudspeakers.
"We are now announcing the winner of our post-game raffle!....
 Claire Thompson, please make your way down to the field to claim your prize!"

I froze, blinking in confusion. *What*?

I had completely forgotten about the raffle to be honest. I barely remembered entering it. Yet here I was, hearing my name echo across the stadium. People around me started pointing, grinning, nudging me toward the aisle.

The crowd's excitement swelled, and my heart began to pound again, this time not from the game but from being suddenly thrust into the spotlight. I stood, still reeling from the win, still trying to catch up with what was happening. Cheering voices urged me forward. I squeezed past students, players, and fans, my eyes scanning the sea of faces as I made my way down to the field.

And then I saw him. Sutton. He was standing near the sidelines, waiting. Even from a distance, his calm posture stood out from the chaos. But there was something about his expression, something focused, almost nervous, that made my stomach flip. When our eyes met, my heart skipped. I walked toward him, trying to steady myself.

Sutton stepped closer, meeting me halfway, his hands tucked into his jacket pockets. "You're looking for your prize?" he asked, his voice low, teasing, but with an undercurrent of something more.

"I-yeah, I guess?" I said, glancing at the field behind us, where the celebration was still roaring.

"I honestly forgot I even entered."

He smiled at that, pulling something from his pocket.

For a second I thought it was going to be an actual raffle prize, but it wasn't.

Instead, it was a small folded card with my name written across the front. He handed it to me. My brow furrowed as I opened it, expecting a gift card or ticket. But instead, scrawled in his handwriting, were the words:

"Will you be my girlfriend, Claire Thompson?"

I blinked at it, then up at him, just to see to my surprise he had the most beautiful assorition of flowers in his hand.

Pink and white peonies.

How, I am still not sure honestly. But once I recollected myself and came into realization again, my heart doing somersaults.

Is this really happening?

Sutton's smile softened, his voice quieter now.

"I know this isn't exactly a normal raffle prize," he said, rubbing the back of his neck. "But you've been with me through everything. Every game, every practice, every crazy moment… and I realized I don't want you just cheering me on from the stands. I want you with me, officially."

The noise of the crowd faded, just a hum in the background. All I could see was Sutton, his nervous eyes locked on mine.

"I want us to be together, Claire," he said, his voice sure now. "Will you be my girlfriend?" He says handing me the flower bouquet.

The noise of the crowd became a distant hum, and all I could hear was the steady beat of my heart and the warmth of his embrace.

"I've got you, Claire," he whispered, his voice full of certainty, "*always*."

And as the stadium continued to cheer around us, I knew this moment wasn't just about the game, the win, or the proposal. It was about us, about everything that had led us here, and everything that was yet to come. With Sutton by my side, I was ready for whatever the future held.

As we stood there, surrounded by the buzzing energy of the crowd, I felt a sense of peace wash over me. The game was over, but the victory I had longed for wasn't just about Sutton's touchdown or the championship, it was about us, about how far we had come together. Our journey had only just begun, and now, we were walking it side by side. Sutton's hand was still in mine, our fingers intertwined as if he never wanted to let go.

I looked up at him, meeting his eyes. There was so much more to say, more than the words that had already been spoken.

"You know," I said softly, almost to myself, "I always thought that the big moments were what mattered most. Graduation, getting the job we wanted, big milestones like this game. But now... I see it differently. It's the small moments, like this one, where I feel truly alive."

Sutton's smile softened as he gently lifted his hand to brush a strand of hair from my face, his touch so tender it made my heart flutter.

"It's the little moments that add up to the big ones, Claire. Every laugh, every challenge we've faced... it's all led us here. And I wouldn't change a thing." He said.

I let out a breath I hadn't realized I was holding. Everything we'd been through, every late-night study session, every moment of doubt, every triumph, and every struggle, had brought us closer. We were no longer just two people navigating college life separately. We were building something bigger, something lasting.

The stadium was starting to empty, the echoes of the victory fading, but the moment between Sutton and me felt eternal. The noise, the cheers, even the flashing lights, all of that began to feel distant, like a dream. What mattered now was this: the love between us and the future we were stepping into, one step at a time. As we walked toward the exit of the field, our hands still linked, I couldn't help but glance up at him again.

"What happens next, Sutton? After all this? After graduation, after everything?"

He looked down at me, his expression thoughtful but full of that unwavering certainty that I had come to know so well.

"We keep moving forward. We trust God, trust each other, and take it one day at a time. No matter what happens, we've got each other. And that's more than enough to get through whatever comes next."

My heart swelled with gratitude. *One day at a time.*

The future was unknown, but with Sutton by my side, I felt ready for it. There was peace in the uncertainty now. We weren't meant to have all the answers yet.

But we were meant to trust the journey, trust each other, and trust God.

As we made our way through the parking lot, hand in hand, the world around us felt different. The usual hustle and bustle, the hum of late-night conversations, the sound of tires on asphalt, it all seemed so distant now.

All that mattered was the presence of each other, the connection we had forged that night. I glanced up at the stars, a vast expanse of possibilities above us, and I couldn't help but feel a sense of awe at how far we had come. The road had been long and uncertain, but it had led me to this, Sutton, standing beside me, ready to face whatever the future held. "You know," I said quietly,

"I never imagined college would be like this. So full of surprises. So full of... us." I said.

Sutton's grip on my hand tightened, a silent promise in his touch. He looked over at me, his eyes reflecting the starlight.

"I'm glad I didn't have to imagine it. I'm glad it's real."

His words were simple, but they held so much weight.

As we walked toward the car, the laughter from the game still echoing faintly in the distance, I realized that the season wasn't over, not for us. There were still moments to be made, still dreams to chase. We weren't just finishing a chapter; we were beginning one. Sutton and I walked together, my mind wandered to the road ahead. We would face new challenges, new decisions about our careers, about where life would take us. But I knew that with Sutton, we would face it all with faith and love as our foundation. We had built something real, something lasting, and now we would nurture it, every single day. Sutton squeezed my hand gently, pulling me from my thoughts.

"I've always known that God had a plan for us, Claire. This, this moment, us, was always meant to be. And I believe with everything I have that we're exactly where we're supposed to be."

I smiled, my heart full.

"I believe that too, Sutton. Every step has led us here. And I can't wait to see where we go next."

As we reached the parking lot exit, almost to my car, Sutton stopped and turned to me, his eyes soft but full of intensity.

"Claire, I meant what I said earlier. I'm with you, every step of the way. You're my person. And I'll do whatever it takes to make sure we're always walking this journey together."

I felt my chest tighten with emotion. I had never felt so certain of anything in my life.

"You'll never be alone, Sutton," I said, my voice steady but full of feeling. "I'm here for you. Always."

We stood there for a moment, letting the words settle between us, before Sutton leaned in and kissed me softly. The kiss was a promise, a promise of everything to come, of everything we had already shared, and of everything we would continue to build together. It was the start of something new and beautiful. And as we pulled away, I knew that no matter what the future held, we would face it together. With God at the center of our relationship, with our love for each other as our guide, and with the trust we had built, there was nothing we couldn't overcome. When we finally arrived at the dorm, we stood by the car for a moment, neither of us in a hurry to leave. It was as if the world had slowed down, and we were just taking it all in, the warmth of the night, the cool breeze, the feeling of everything falling into place.

"You know, I've been thinking," I began, my thoughts spilling out without warning, "about what you said earlier, about taking it one day at a time."

Sutton looked at me, his eyes kind and patient, as if waiting for me to continue.

"I think you're right. There's so much we can't control, but as long as we're together, I'm ready for it. Whatever comes next, we'll figure it out."

He smiled, the corners of his eyes crinkling in that way that always made my heart race.

"We're in this together, Claire. Always."

The words hung in the air between us, like a promise, an unspoken understanding that everything was going to be okay as long as we had each other. And with that, I knew, deep down, that no matter what the future held, we would face it with courage, faith, and love as our guiding lights.

The journey was just beginning, and I was ready to walk it with Sutton by my side.

22

The sun was setting behind the campus as I stood with Sutton, both of us dressed in our caps and gowns.

The day had finally arrived, the day we had worked so hard for. Graduation. The culmination of years of hard work, sleepless nights, and countless memories.

The atmosphere was alive with excitement, but as I glanced at Sutton, I felt a peace that went beyond the celebrations around us. We had come so far since that unforgettable night in the stadium. From the moment he asked me to be his girlfriend, our journey had been one of growth, love, and faith. We had learned to lean on each other, to support one another through the ups and downs, and to trust that God had a plan for us, one that was unfolding in His perfect timing. Sutton's hand was resting gently on mine as we walked toward the stage, the cheers of our classmates and families echoing in the background.

It felt surreal to be standing here with him, knowing that we were about to take the next step into a new chapter of our lives. The excitement of graduation was still there, but it wasn't the end of the story. It was just the beginning.

After the ceremony, we found a quiet spot near the campus fountain, the place where we had spent countless hours studying, talking, and dreaming about the future.

The sun's golden rays cast a warm glow over everything, and for a moment, it felt like time had slowed down, as though the world had paused just for us.

"I can't believe we're here," I said, my voice full of awe. "It feels like just yesterday we were freshmen, trying to figure it all out."

Sutton smiled, his eyes full of tenderness.

"I know. And now, look at us. You're going to be a NICU nurse, and I'm about to start med school. We've come a long way."

I nodded, the weight of the moment settling over me. We had both worked tirelessly to get to this point, and now, we were ready to pursue our dreams. Sutton's journey toward becoming a doctor and mine toward nursing were just the start of the lives we had imagined together. But what mattered most was that we had each other, and we had the faith to guide us forward.

"Remember when we prayed for guidance, for clarity?" I said softly. "I think God has been guiding us every step of the way."

Sutton's smile deepened as he pulled me closer.

 "I've always believed that. And I believe that everything we've been through, every challenge, every triumph, was part of His plan for us."

We stood there, side by side, taking in the beauty of the campus and the future that lay ahead. The road wasn't always going to be easy, but we had built something strong, our relationship, our faith, and our dreams, and we knew that together, we could face anything that came our way. Sutton glanced over at me again, a slight smile on his face.

"You know, there's something I've been thinking about since that night in the stadium."

I raised an eyebrow, curious. "What do you mean?"

 He hesitated for a moment, his eyes focusing on the road ahead.

 "I remember when I asked you to be my girlfriend. It felt like a big leap, but now... it feels like it was just the beginning of something so much bigger. I look at everything we've been through together, and it's clear to me that we were always meant to be. This, this moment we're living in right now, is exactly where we're supposed to be."

My heart swelled with emotion as I processed his words.

"I know exactly what you mean. I never could have imagined everything that would come after that. But I wouldn't change a single thing. Not one moment."

Sutton's voice softened. "Neither would I. Every late-night study session, every quiet walk we took, every prayer we shared, it all led us to this moment. And now that we're here, I'm more certain than ever that this is just the start of something incredible."

I looked at him, the love and certainty in his eyes making me feel like everything was going to be okay. No matter what the future held, we were in this together. As the evening drew to a close, we made our way to the car, our hearts full of hope for the future. The world was open to us, and we were ready to step into it, hand in hand, with faith as our compass. As we drove away from the campus, the city lights twinkling ahead of us, Sutton reached for my hand, his fingers gently curling around mine. I looked over at him, seeing the love and certainty in his eyes.

"We've got this, Claire," he said, his voice steady and filled with love. "We've always had it, as long as we have each other and God at the center of everything."

I smiled, squeezing his hand.

"I know. Whatever happens, we'll face it together."

The car hummed along the road, and for a moment, everything felt right. The uncertainty of the future no longer felt daunting. Instead, it felt like an exciting adventure, one that we would embark on together.

And as we drove toward the future, I whispered softly, a prayer in my heart, knowing that everything was exactly as it was meant to be.

"God, thank you for this journey. Thank you for Sutton. Thank you for Your timing."

Sutton turned to me, a soft smile playing on his lips. The road stretched out before us, the quiet hum of the car filling the space between us. The world outside was a blur of city lights and shadows, but inside, there was nothing but peace. I leaned my head against the window, watching the night sky unfold above us. A thousand thoughts swirled in my mind, dreams, hopes, uncertainties, but amidst it all, there was a sense of calm that I couldn't quite explain. It wasn't just because of Sutton's presence beside me; it was the quiet assurance that God had us exactly where we needed to be. Sutton glanced over at me, his expression soft but serious.

"Claire, do you ever wonder how we got here? How everything just seemed to fall into place?"

I smiled at the thought, my heart swelling at the question.

"All the time. I think about how we've grown, how we've been able to support each other in ways I never imagined. And then I remember everything we've been through together, the late nights, the hard days, and it all feels like it led us here. To this moment."

Sutton nodded, his fingers still gently holding mine.

"I think we've been through it all for a reason. I used to think that things had to happen on my own terms, but I've realized now that God's plan is always better than anything I could've imagined."

I couldn't help but agree. It was something I had learned over time, that trust in His timing was everything. When things seemed uncertain, when the path ahead felt unclear, it was the knowledge that He had a bigger plan that kept me going.

"As much as I've dreamed about becoming a doctor," Sutton continued, "there's something even more important I've learned these past few years. And that's that I'm not in control of everything. But God is. And with you by my side, I know we can face anything."

I squeezed his hand tighter, my heart full of gratitude.

"I feel the same way. Every step has been leading us toward this moment, but it's more than just graduation, more than just starting our careers. It's about the journey we're going to take together. With you, I feel like we can do anything."

We drove in silence for a while, each of us reflecting on our individual journeys, on everything we had learned and experienced in our time at UNC. The challenges, the growth, and the moments of clarity. And yet, even with all that, the most important thing remained clear: our shared future. We were no longer two individuals heading in separate directions, but a pair with a shared purpose and a shared dream. Sutton's voice broke the silence again.

"Have you thought about where we'll be a year from now? What our lives will look like?"

I couldn't help but smile at his question.

"I've thought about it. But honestly, I'm not focused on the exact details. I'm focused on knowing that no matter where we are, we'll be together. And that makes all the difference."

He laughed softly, his eyes lighting up with affection.

"You're right. I've never been so sure about anything in my life as I am about us. The future doesn't scare me anymore." "And it shouldn't," I added. "Because we've got each other, and with God guiding us, there's nothing to fear. Whatever comes next, we'll face it together."

As we continued to drive, the weight of graduation began to sink in. We had made it through the challenges of college, the stress of exams, the uncertainty of our futures, and now, we were stepping into the next chapter. But even though it was a milestone, it didn't feel like an ending. It felt like the beginning of something even more profound. When we arrived back at our apartment, we sat on the couch, the quiet of the night wrapping around us. There was a quiet assurance that came over me as I sat next to Sutton, knowing that our journey wasn't defined by any one moment. It was the small moments, the quiet conversations, the shared dreams and prayers, that had brought us here.

And now, standing on the edge of a new chapter, I knew that we would continue to grow, continue to learn, and continue to walk hand in hand.

"You're right," I whispered, more to myself than to Sutton. "We've been through so much already, and I know that whatever comes next, we'll face it together. With God by our side, I know we're ready for whatever comes."

Sutton kissed my hand softly, and said "I'm with you every step of the way, Claire. And with God at the center of everything, I believe there's nothing we can't handle."

The words settled in my heart like a prayer, and in that moment, I felt more certain than ever that our love, our faith, and our trust in each other would carry us through anything that lay ahead. There was so much we had to look forward to, his medical school, my work as a NICU nurse, but there was also a comfort in knowing that we had already built something strong. Our relationship wasn't based solely on dreams or ambitions. It was rooted in faith, in trust, and in the unwavering belief that God had a plan for us. Sutton shifted, facing me with a tender smile.

"I know we've talked about our futures, but Claire, I want you to know that no matter where life takes us, I'll always be there. I'm not just committed to you for today or tomorrow, I'm committed for the long haul. We've got a lifetime ahead of us."

Tears welled up in my eyes at his words. The love I felt for him was more than I could put into words.

"I believe that too, Sutton. And I'll always be there for you, no matter what. Together, we'll face everything that comes our way."

With that, Sutton leaned in, his lips brushing mine in a soft, heartfelt kiss to my hand once again. It was a soft kiss that spoke volumes, of everything we had been through, of everything we had become, and of the many more moments we would share in the future. Sutton's words were simple, yet they filled my heart with a certainty I had never known before. With God at the center, there was nothing we couldn't handle. I looked at Sutton, and it hit me again, this wasn't the end, but the beginning. We were exactly where we were meant to be, and with God's timing, I knew He would lead us forward, step by step. And I knew that, no matter what, we would always be there for each other. As we pulled away, I smiled, feeling an overwhelming sense of peace. The future no longer felt uncertain or overwhelming. With Sutton by my side, and with God at the center of everything we did, I knew we could face whatever came next. And as I whispered a silent prayer of gratitude, I felt a deep sense of trust. Trust that everything, every step, every challenge, and every victory, was all part of His plan.

"Claire," Sutton said softly, his voice filled with certainty,

"It's all in His timing."

EPILOGUE

A year had passed since that quiet moment in the fading light, when Sutton and I had found certainty in each other's eyes, with God's guiding hand ever present in our hearts. The road hadn't always been easy, life had its twists, and our dreams had taken us down paths we hadn't always expected. But through it all, we had held tight to one another, and more importantly, to our faith. Sutton had entered medical school with a quiet resolve, his passion for healing and his drive to serve others only growing stronger. There were long nights of studying, moments of self-doubt, but through it all, I had seen him become the doctor he had always dreamed of becoming. And I had been by his side, cheering him on, trusting that God's timing was, once again, perfect. As for me, I had started my journey as a NICU nurse, surrounded by tiny, precious lives every day. There was a deep sense of fulfillment in knowing that I was doing what I had always dreamed of, comforting the most vulnerable. But even more, I had discovered a new strength in myself, a strength that came from knowing my worth was never defined by the challenges I faced but by the love and grace God had poured into my life. But it was in those quiet moments, after the noise of the world had faded, that we truly found the depth of our relationship. I had watched Sutton go through the intense pressures of med school, and through it all, we had leaned on each other and on God. And now, it seemed like we were approaching another milestone, our own family. It all started when we began to talk about starting that family, and Sutton, ever patient and supportive, was always willing to listen, to pray with me, and to trust that God's timing would guide us in this. Together, we prayed for the right moment. It wasn't easy waiting, but we knew in our hearts that God had a plan. Days, weeks, and months passed, but our trust never wavered. And then came that bright Sunday morning, when everything changed. At 2:30 a.m., I found myself vomiting in the bathroom. I told Sutton, and he handed me a pregnancy test. My hands were trembling as I held the test, waiting those endless three minutes. When the test finally revealed two pink lines, our hearts soared. We were expecting our first child, and we had never been more overjoyed. Our prayers had been answered. It was more than a dream, it was a reality. Not only was I eating for one, but now, I was eating for two. It wasn't long after we found out we were expecting a baby girl, that the next piece of our journey began unfolding. Sutton's face lit up with happiness, and I couldn't help but smile as we imagined our little girl joining us in June. It was incredible, our relationship, our dreams, our future, it was all coming together, part of God's perfect plan for us. Our love had only deepened over time. We had faced challenges together, unexpected moves, busy schedules, moments of doubt, but with each trial, we had learned to trust each other more and to trust God more deeply. Our love wasn't perfect, but it was real, and it was rooted in something stronger than ourselves. There were days when life seemed overwhelming, when the weight of responsibilities felt heavy, but we had learned to pause, to pray, and to remind each other that it was all part of the plan. We often found ourselves reflecting on how far we had come, and it wasn't always the grand moments that mattered most. It was the small moments, the shared smiles, the quiet prayers, the simple gestures of love, that truly defined us. Through all the noise, those moments of connection, of holding each other in faith, became the foundation of our relationship. Sutton and I had seen the hand of God in our journey, not just in the big decisions, but in the little things, the way our paths crossed, the timing of our meeting, and how we were always led exactly where we needed to be. We learned that life wasn't about having all the answers, it was about trusting in the One who held them. Even when things didn't make sense, we trusted that His timing was perfect. As we looked toward the future, there was no fear, only hope. The road ahead remained unknown, but we had each other, and more importantly, we had faith. We had the certainty that whatever came next, it would be part of God's plan. No matter the challenges or the victories, the moments of doubt or the leaps of faith, we knew we were exactly where we were meant to be. Together, with God at the center, we had learned that love was not just something we felt, it was something we lived, with each new step we took, trusting in His timing. And now, as we prepared to welcome our little girl into the world, I knew with every ounce of my being that the best was yet to come. We were standing on the threshold of a new chapter, our hearts full, hands clasped, and ready to face whatever life had in store for us. This journey was just beginning. Our story, God's story for us, was unfolding in ways we couldn't have imagined. Every moment, every step was a reminder that His timing was perfect. And together, we would face whatever was next, hand in hand, with God guiding us every step of the way.

 We were ready for the beautiful, messy, and wonderful adventure of life ahead, knowing that through everything, the best was yet to come.

Thank you's!

There are so many people who have helped shape this journey and made this book possible. I owe so much to those who have been there for me, supporting me, guiding me, and offering unwavering love. I have been dreaming of writing books for as long as I can remember, and have always had an advanced talent of written in school. First and foremost, I want to thank God for guiding me throughout this entire journey. Without His presence in my life, I wouldn't have had the strength, clarity, or inspiration to pursue this path. He has led me every step of the way, and it is through His grace that this book came to fruition. I am deeply grateful for His guidance, His love, and His unending faithfulness as I navigated the challenges of writing this piece. Every word, every moment of inspiration, was made possible because of Him. To my mom: You have been my anchor throughout this entire process. Your constant encouragement and belief in me kept me going, even during the times when I felt like giving up. Thank you for always reminding me of my strength and potential. Your love is unwavering, and your faith in me helped me find the courage to keep pushing forward. I love you more than words can express, and I am so blessed to have you by my side. To my dad: Your pride in me has been a constant source of motivation. From the moment I began this journey, your belief in my abilities has fueled me to keep going. Knowing that you are proud of me has been a reminder that I am on the right path. Thank you for being my biggest supporter and for always encouraging me to aim higher. I love you so much, and I am so grateful to have you in my life. To my sister: Your words of love and pride have meant everything to me. Whenever I doubted myself, you were always there to remind me of how far I've come and what I'm capable of. Your encouragement has been a beacon of light during moments of uncertainty, and I am so thankful for you. You've always believed in me, and for that, I love you endlessly. Your support has been invaluable, and I am lucky to have you by my side. And lastly, a special thank you to Brandi Berry, the author of two phenomenal books, *Wildfire* and *Written*. Brandi, your help in revising my work and boosting my confidence throughout the writing process has been instrumental. Your insight, expertise, and encouragement were exactly what I needed to bring my vision to life. I couldn't have asked for a better guide during this journey. Your belief in my potential helped me believe in myself, and I am deeply grateful for all the ways you've supported me. Your talent and generosity of spirit have made such a lasting impact on me, and I'm honored to have had the opportunity to learn from you. To all of you. My Lord, my family, and Brandi, thank you for being my foundation. Your love, pride, and support have shaped me into the person I am today. This book is as much yours as it is mine, and I will forever be grateful for the ways you've helped me grow. I love you all beyond words, and I will always carry your encouragement with me! Can not thank you all enough! God bless!

About the Author

She is a high school student with a deep passion for her love for God, writing and golf. When she's not attending school, you'll most likely find her on the golf course, working relentlessly toward her college golf dreams. Whether it's perfecting her swing or strategizing for her next match, golf has always been a major part of her last couple years. But when she's not hitting the greens, she is at home, in front of her laptop, or notebook, writing the stories that have been brewing in her mind for years. Though she has always dreamed of becoming a writer, the fear of judgment once held her back. She was unsure of how others would think of her work. But her love for storytelling, and impressive scores on writing exams ultimately led her to share her first novel, a project that has been years in the making. She hopes that her debut novel resonates with readers and serves as the first step in her writing journey, with many more books to come. Beyond writing and golf, she is obsessed with Alani energy drinks, coffee, and time spent on the golf course. Above all, she treasures the time spent with her small, close-knit family, her mom, dad, and sister, who have supported her every step of the way. As she looks ahead to the future, she is excited to continue exploring her passion for writing and sharing more of her stories with the world

www.ingramcontent.com/pod-product-compliance
Lightning Source LLC
Chambersburg PA
CBHW050702290626
47170CB00016B/2585